everything I was

everything I was

Corinne Demas

 Carolrhoda LAB

MINNEAPOLIS

Carolrhoda Lab™
An imprint of Carolrhoda Books
A division of Lerner Publishing Group, Inc.
241 First Avenue North
Minneapolis, MN 55401 U.S.A.

Website address: www.lernerbooks.com

The images in this book are used with the permission of: Front cover:.
© RubberBall/Alamy (woman swimming); back cover: © iStockphoto.com/
eli_asenova (waves); jacket flaps: © iStockphoto.com/ nicholas belton (cardboard).
Interior: © iStockphoto.com/ Alex Potemkin (rings on water), half title page;
iStockphoto.com/eli_asenova (waves), throughout interior; © iStockphoto.com/
nicholas belton (cardboard), throughout interior.

Library of Congress Cataloging-in-Publication Data

Demas, Corinne.
        Everything I was / by Corinne Demas.
            p.   cm.
        Summary: Thirteen-year-old Irene helps in her grandfather's plant nursery, makes new friends, and begins to learn what she really wants and needs after her father, having lost his job as an investment banker, moves her and her mother to his father's farmhouse upstate.
        ISBN: 978-0-7613-7303-2 (trade hard cover : alk. paper)
        [1. Family problems—Fiction. 2. Moving, Household—Fiction.
3. Grandfathers—Fiction. 4. Friendship—Fiction. 5. Nurseries (Horticulture)—
Fiction. 6. Family life—New York—Fiction. 7. New York (State)—Fiction.] I. Title.
PZ7.D39145My 2011
[Fic]—dc22   2010027374

Manufactured in the United States of America
1 – SB – 12/31/10

FOR ELAINE

chapter one

They dismantled my brass canopy bed and carried it out, a man in front and a man in back. Another moving man, fat, with a red beard, grabbed my beanbag chair and lugged it away. I closed my eyes for a minute, and imagined that when I opened them my room would look right again, the way I had always known it, with the furniture where it belonged, the curtains on the windows, and my posters on the walls. But it didn't work. My walls were stripped, and all that was left in the room was a pile of boxes and my mattress propped against the wall. The two men came back for the mattress, and the one with the red beard hoisted two liquor-store boxes, piled one on top of the other.

"What you got in here, honey?" he asked, laughing. "Rocks?"

No sooner had he asked than the bottom of one box split open and a pile of magazines I'd been saving gushed out over the floor. My mom was coming into the room at just that moment.

"I told you to get rid of those," she said. "We're not paying for storage in Manhattan so you can keep old magazines."

"Throw them out, then," I cried. "Throw out everything of mine."

I went out on the terrace and looked out over the city— a view I knew by heart, but might never see exactly this way again. I shut my eyes again and held them shut. When I opened them, the view was there, untouched.

It was sunny on the terrace, but cool. I sat on the tile floor, out of the wind. The wrought-iron furniture had been sold at auction, along with the rugs and antiques, but the wooden planters were still there, a few sprigs of weeds growing bravely in the dirt. Since we knew we were going to be leaving, there hadn't seemed much point in planting pansies and petunias this spring.

After a while my dad came out on the terrace and sat beside me. His legs were so long his feet nearly touched the other side.

"Your mother's directing operations quite well without my help," he said. "I thought I'd best keep out of the way."

I leaned back against the warm brick wall and looked up at the sky.

My dad leaned back too.

"This is just a temporary move, sweetheart," he said. "A retrenching. I'll get another job, we'll get our finances under control, and everything will work out OK."

"We're never coming back to this apartment, though, are we?"

"No, not here," he said. "We'll find something not so expensive, but something nice," he added.

"Am I going back to my school?"

"I'm not sure," he said.

"I don't want to go back if I have to be on scholarship," I said. "It's awful, having everyone know."

"No one would know."

"They'll know," I said.

One of the movers stuck his head out onto the terrace.

"We taking anything from out here?"

"No," my dad said. "Nothing here to take."

The terrace door closed hard.

"I'm sorry about all this, sweetheart," my dad said. "You can't imagine how sorry I am."

He lifted his arm and put it around me. His hand cupped my shoulder and he pulled me gently against him. But even though I wanted to lean in against him, I didn't let myself. I sat up as straight as I could and studied the railing of the terrace. It was only after he got up and went back inside the apartment that I sank forward, pressed my face against my knees, and let myself cry.

chapter two

It had happened slowly at first, the change in our lives. The first time I was aware there was anything wrong was when my dad said he wanted to cancel our February vacation.

"This isn't a good time," he told my mom. I thought, at first, he was talking about the chance of rotten weather. My dad hates flying, and inevitably when we fly somewhere in the winter we end up on a plane that gets rerouted, and we have to camp out in some bleak airport to wait for an even smaller plane that takes off in a blizzard.

"I think it's important," my mom argued. "We need this vacation, God knows we need it."

"But it's not prudent," my dad said. "Not now."

"I'm sick of prudent," said my mom.

"I haven't seen much sign of that," said my dad.

But my mom must have won my dad over, because we went.

The whole plane ride down my dad didn't even dart a look out the window. He gripped the armrests, and stared, instead, at the seat back in front of him. If I hadn't known his views on religion I would have thought he was locked in prayer, but in fact he was working hard to be stoic. My mom loves flying, and while the turbulence we hit made my dad clench his teeth, she was like a little kid on an amusement park ride.

"Don't worry about your father," she told me. "He'll cheer up as soon as we get there and he relaxes in the sunshine."

But my dad didn't relax, and he didn't cheer up. When she finally got him into a bathing suit and out on a chaise lounge on the beach, he lay there like he was in the airplane, waiting for it to take off.

"You've got to come in," my mom urged him. "The water's gorgeous, darling."

"I'm fine where I am," my dad said.

"Tell him how warm it is, Irene," my mom said.

"It's warm, Daddy," I said, but without much conviction.

"I'm glad," my dad said.

"It won't cost you any more to get wet," my mom said. But my dad wouldn't respond.

"Well, Irene, you and I will enjoy this gorgeous ocean even if your father has decided not to." And she took my hand and pulled me along back into the water. "Let's do handstands," she said. "Let's see who can stay up longer."

My mom was good at handstands. She'd been a competitive diver in college and she could keep her legs perfectly straight, her feet close together, toes pointed. She had small, pretty feet that she was proud of—mine were already a size bigger—and she kept her toenails as filed and polished as if they were fingernails.

I could tell she was determined to make us feel we were enjoying ourselves, in spite of my dad, but every time I looked back at the shore there he was, positioned on the chaise, stoic as he'd been on the airplane.

The next day, my dad suggested that we pick up some food and make dinner in our condo, but my mom insisted we eat at the club dining room. The place we rented had a tiny kitchen, with everything cleverly designed to be compact. I thought it would be fun to use it, like playing house.

"This is a vacation," my mom argued. "We're not doing any cooking."

"I was thinking of something easy," my dad said.

"It's a vacation," my mom said. "I want to dress up. I want to eat out." She looked over at me, and I wished I had ducked out of sight before the argument had started. "Put on something nicer, Irene," she said. "This is dinner."

"I'm not wearing a dress."

"You can at least put on a nice top. And brush your hair back so we can see your face."

"This is a nice top," I said, but my mom gave me one of her firm looks, so I went and changed into a shirt I hated, one she'd bought for me and made me bring. It seemed easier that way.

At dinner my dad tried to order an omelet, but was forced to order an entire dinner. He folded up the wine menu in its leather folder and handed it back to the waiter.

"We're not having any, thank you," he said. My mom leaned forward, about to protest, but then sat back in her chair, her lips tight.

After the salads were served the waiter came around with a pepper grinder. "Would you like some fresh ground pepper?" he asked.

My dad waved him away.

"I would like some," my mom said in a firm voice, and the waiter, with a glance at my dad, timidly approached my mom's plate. The pepper landed like gnats on the fringes of the lettuce leaves.

The waiter was barely out of earshot before my dad said, "I don't understand these restaurants. Why can't they just leave a pepper grinder at each table. If I want pepper I am certainly capable of grinding it myself."

"Maybe it's because the pepper grinder's so big," I said. "It would take up too much room on the table."

"So who needs a pepper grinder the size of a billy club?" my dad asked.

When the entrées arrived, my mom dug into hers with relish, praising, extravagantly, everything on her plate. My dad only plucked at his dinner.

"It won't cost you any less, Leland, if you leave food on your plate."

"I should never have let you talk me into this," my dad said, and I wasn't sure if he meant the pink glistening salmon, studded with capers, on the table before him, eating out in this fancy restaurant, or the vacation as a whole.

chapter three

The desk in our condo was outfitted with a port-folio of tourist information and a writing folder with stationery and postcards. There were two post-card choices: a view of the white, stucco buildings against the blue sky, striped umbrellas on every terrace, or a view of the ocean with a couple, in outdated bathing suits, walking along the sand.

I had gotten Mr. McClure's home address before we left and marked it in my address book with just his initials, G. M. It was amazing to me that he had been there in the telephone book, just like any other person, all along. We had an unlisted number, as did many of my friends' parents. I had expected teachers would too. It would be possible to walk right along his street, right past his building, and see where he lived. While my parents were sleeping late, I went out onto the terrace with the writing folder. I studied both postcards. Neither of them was right, but I settled on the one with the ocean, since that was the view from where I sat.

But what should I write? "Wish you were here" is what one always wrote. That was true, of course, but what I really wished for was an improved version of here—here, this place, but without my parents hovering around. Here, but with me older and on my own.

I flipped through the stationery. A letter would be private. But a letter would require me to produce something more than a breezy hello, and what would I say? A letter seemed too important. He might take it all wrong. I pulled out the postcard again.

But how to begin? "Dear Mr. McClure" sounded so formal, but I could hardly use his first name—would I write Richard or Rich? He was interested in birds, I knew that. So, skipping the salutation, I began: "There are gulls here, graceful, with long tails (they're called "longtails"); they look like rare birds, but they're common as our gulls." That seemed safe, but it sounded pretty dumb.

I hadn't heard my mom come out on the terrace behind me. So she startled me when she spoke. "Are you writing to Jenna?" she asked.

My hand went instantly to cover my words, before I realized that there was nothing in them to give me away.

"Sure," I said, "I'm writing to her."

Jenna was my sister—half sister, to be exact. She was a grad student, living near her father and his wife in Wyoming.

It seemed so much easier, then, to be writing to Jenna. I felt flooded by relief. It had probably been a stupid idea to send a card to Mr. McClure. Stupid, or worse.

On top of my comment about the birds I wrote, "Dear Jenna."

Underneath I wrote, "We're having a great time."

"Say hello for me," said my mom. And so I added, "Mom says hello."

"Say hello to Peter and Davida, also," said my mom, and she went inside before she could see that I had decided not to add that.

I'd met Jenna's father and his wife the year before, when they had come East for a conference. It was impossible to imagine that my mom had ever been married to Peter. He was a geologist, a small man who wore itchy-looking wool clothes and had an itchy-looking beard and bristly hair. His wife, Davida (the first syllable pronounced like "day," she reminded my mom several times), was also small, with frizzy hair, and she too wore itchy-looking clothes. My mom was wearing a peach-colored silk blouse and a sleek, grey skirt, while they, in their brown tweeds, looked like two burrs that would stick together.

My mom had gone to great trouble readying the apartment for their visit—fresh flowers in her best vases, magazines symmetrically arranged, books (that she had bought because she felt she should read them, but in most likelihood never would) artistically stacked. But I could tell in a minute that her efforts to impress them were pointless. Neither Peter nor Davida were people who noticed or cared about such things.

I had thought my mom had left Peter for my dad— my dad who was tall and handsome and ambitious in a worldly way. (Or was he? Maybe it was just my mom who was ambitious.) But Peter hardly acted like a man who had been scorned. His attitude toward my mom was that of an old friend one has outgrown. Davida, also a geologist, was clearly a woman who shared his interests and his style. They seemed so well suited to each other my mom seemed more like a mistake of Peter's past than a partner he had regretted losing.

"Why did you marry Peter?" I asked her later.

"I met him in college," she said. "He was intelligent and dedicated. He seemed so certain about things. So grown up." She gave a little laugh. "I had no idea what I wanted from life. He was quite clear about what he wanted. I was attracted by that. It just took me a few years to figure out that what he wanted wasn't at all what I did."

"Are you sorry you married him?"

"No, how could I be?" asked my mom. "If I hadn't married him I wouldn't have had Jenna."

"Are you sorry you didn't stay married to him?"

My mom looked hard at me. "Of course not," she said.

chapter four

My dad came home from our vacation as pale as the day he left. My mom returned tan and radiant. She was always worrying about skin cancer and had brought a huge collection of sunscreen with us, yet she was inconsistent enough to be pleased when she "bronzed nicely" and told me I looked so much better when I had "a little color" in my face.

We had been home a week, our tans almost faded, when my dad announced to my mom at dinner that the merger had finally taken place.

Whenever my parents talked about business things—like mergers—I usually stopped paying attention to their conversation. That night I happened to be looking at my mom's face when my dad said this. She gave a little blink of alarm, and her tongue darted around her upper lip, searching nervously for invisible stray crumbs.

"They'll begin downsizing immediately," my dad said.

"I doubt it," said my mom.

"Watch."

"What's downsizing?" I asked.

My dad turned to me. "It means 'make smaller'," he said. "When a company wants to cut down on spending, they eliminate a lot of people's jobs."

"Not yours," my mom said firmly. "You're a vice president; they can't eliminate yours."

"They're looking to save money," my dad said. "It's the people with the biggest salaries who'll be axed first."

"Don't listen to him," my mom said, turning to me. "Your father's job is perfectly secure. There's nothing to worry about."

My dad had been holding the lid of the glass butter dish. He set it back down, glass against glass, then pushed it away from his place.

"I don't want you to be worrying," he said to me. "But things are rather uncertain now." He looked over at my mom. "It wouldn't hurt if this family started practicing some serious economizing."

My mom reached forward and touched the vase of flowers in the center of the table. "Daisies," she said, playfully. "We'll have daisies from now on. These will be our last freesias, our last roses, our last delphiniums." She looked over at my dad and laughed.

It was always my mom who laughed at things first. My mom who prodded my dad until he shared in her amusement, smiled along with her. Now his face remained solemn. My mom's hand moved from the vase to my dad's forearm, but still he didn't smile. Finally, she got up out of her seat and went behind my dad's chair and leaned over to kiss him.

"Daisies?" she asked.

At last, my dad smiled. He reached up and took her arms and pulled her around to kiss her.

And then, once things were restored between them, I felt I could leave the table and go to my room to work on my homework.

chapter five

My mom was wrong about my dad's job, though. He did lose it.

"There's nothing to worry about," she told me brightly. "Daddy will have no trouble finding another one."

But she was wrong about that too.

I listened now to the kinds of conversations I had never followed before. I listened when I wasn't supposed to be listening, when my parents were talking in the kitchen after they thought I had gone to sleep. I listened when my mom was talking on the phone to her friends. She did not confide in them; she kept up a brave front, as if by pretending to them that nothing was going on she could believe it herself. It was her lies that frightened me the most.

"Leland's doing consulting now," she told one friend. "He really wanted more flexibility than he'd had at Bryce-Morehouse. He's so much happier now."

She said this so brightly that at first I thought she must have been talking about some other man, not my dad. My dad, who looked, more and more, like a man who had never been happy in his life.

One night, at dinner, I noticed a new picture on the wall over the sideboard. It was a scene of a little farmhouse at the end of a country road.

"Where'd that come from?" I asked.

"Just a print that I'd never hung before," my mom said.

My mom had a closet full of paintings, drawings, and etchings, some framed, some in portfolios. She had a degree in art history and did volunteer work as a docent at the museum. She liked to think of herself as an art collector.

"What was there before?" I asked.

"A drawing by Caravaggio."

I remembered it then. It was a drawing of a man's face, done with hundreds of fine pencil lines, an old man with a skullcap on his head and a long beard. "Where'd that go?" I asked.

"We auctioned it at Sotheby's," my dad said.

"Sold it? Why?"

"It was worth a great deal of money."

"Did you make a lot on it?" I asked.

I looked over at my mom. She was pressing her lips tightly together.

"Not what we had hoped," said my dad. "It's not a seller's market right now."

I was about to say something like, "Then why did you sell it?"—but I cut myself short. "Well, I like this one better," I said. "It's more colorful."

My mom smiled, a smile to please me. It fell away quickly from her face.

I looked back up at the print. The cottage in the distance had a thatched roof and a thick chimney. The dirt road curved up to it, leading you there. It was the kind of cottage you'd long to enter. I could imagine the inside: a rocking chair by the fire, a painted cupboard, a cozy bed, a place where everything was simple and safe. The surrounding fields would provide for you forever, with all you'd ever need to live.

For three nights in a row I set my alarm for 1 A.M. and called Jenna in Wyoming. I didn't leave a message on her machine, but finally, on the third night, I got her at home.

"What's going on?" I asked her.

"Don't they tell you anything?"

"Well, I know what happened to Daddy's job, but I thought they gave you money when you were fired, so it wouldn't matter all that much."

"Well, they do, to some extent—"Jenna began. "But they took a bath on the stock market and—"

"And what?" I asked.

"They have huge debts."

"How come?"

"It's the way they live. They've been overextended for years. Mom wanted that penthouse and now they can't pay for it."

"But I thought they bought it."

"They have a mortgage, Irene, and there's co-op fees, upkeep, insurance."

"Oh," I said.

"I'm sorry, honey," said Jenna. "Has it been awful for you?"

"No, not really. It's just that I don't know what's going to happen next. I feel like . . . well, I feel like everything's unraveling around me, and I can't stop it."

✳ ✳ ✳

The cleaning service came only every other week now, and my dad took to vacuuming.

"I hate to see you doing that," my mom said.

"It's good exercise," my dad said. "I like it." And it was strange, but he seemed to. In fact, he was better than the cleaners ever were. He moved the sofas in the living room and vacuumed places they had never touched. He found a quarter, several dimes, and a sterling silver button from my mom's jacket cuff.

My mom gave up her health club membership, but bought a Nordic Track machine for herself and an exercise bike for my dad. He said he'd never use it, and he didn't. My mom used them both, defiantly, every day for the first week, but less and less as time went on. It wasn't long before both machines were silent—two skeletons in the corner of the guest room. My mom gave up having her hair done once a week, but used the money she saved to buy a pair of shoes.

"I couldn't resist them," she said, twirling her foot to show me.

"It's not like you needed shoes," I said. My mom could have worn a different pair of shoes every day in the month and not run out.

"Now don't go sounding like your father, Irene," she said. "Nobody needs shoes for their feet. These are shoes for the soul."

☀ ☀ ☀

I had always been a fairly good student at school, but I started getting obsessed about perfect grades. It seemed like the only thing that I could do on my own, the only thing I had any control over. But I didn't have control. I got As on my papers, but although I studied hard for tests, I forgot things I had studied or made ridiculous mistakes. I'd look at my returned test papers and couldn't understand why I had forgotten what I had forgotten, or misunderstood the question, or not seen that I'd put the decimal point in the wrong place. It was as if some other girl who didn't have her head screwed on right was taking those tests in my place.

When Mr. McClure handed back the social studies test that I failed, I burst into tears. I'd thought we were supposed to choose one of three topics, and I'd written an essay on the causes of the Peloponnesian War. Mr. McClure had written "excellent, thoughtful" in the margins of the essay. But I'd read the directions wrong; we were supposed to write on two of the three choices.

He caught me before I was able to duck out of the classroom.

"Come by after school," he said.

Ordinarily this would have made my day. I was always looking for excuses to hang around after class or to see Mr. McClure after school. But it was different now. I'd never done badly on anything for his class before.

"Don't worry, Irene," he said when I turned up at his office. "You've had a great average going into this exam, and one test isn't going to make that much difference."

"I'd really studied for this test, and then I missed a whole essay question."

"Tests aren't all that important, Irene," said Mr. McClure. "What's important is what you get out of the course."

"But I totally screwed up," I said.

"Don't be so hard on yourself," he said.

I didn't know what to say to that. Mr. McClure's face was so handsome, so kind, I couldn't bear to look at him. I stared at his desk. He had a dozen mugs clustered on his desk. Some looked as if they had been used for coffee, but not been washed; others held pens and pencils. The one I gave him still had some candy canes left from Christmas.

In our school, we weren't allowed to give teachers expensive gifts, but mugs were OK. I bet Mr. McClure had several dozen more at home.

"You know, Irene, I've been wondering about you recently," he said. "You seem to be putting a lot of pressure on yourself. School doesn't have to be like this—it shouldn't be like this."

I looked up at him. He was looking straight at me.

"I know," I said, too softly. He leaned forward to hear me. "I know," I said, again, louder.

"Is everything all right at home?" he asked me.

And because I couldn't trust myself not to spill out everything to him, I answered quickly, my voice as bright and cheerful as my mom's.

"Everything's fine," I said. "Everything is just fine."

chapter six

My two best friends, Eve and Frankie, were sleeping over the night after my dad told me about the move. We'd laid out our sleeping bags in the den so we could watch videos on the large screen there. It was after midnight. Frankie had fallen asleep during the second movie, but Eve and I were still awake long after it was over.

"Want some ice cream?" I asked.

"I'm not really hungry," whispered Eve, "but I'll have a little."

Frankie was sleeping on her back, making little blowing noises as she breathed. She had curly red hair and freckles, but in the darkened room her freckles were invisible; her hair had no color. Eve and I tiptoed past her and through the dining room to the kitchen. Eve was wearing grey fleece pj's, and she looked like a kid in an animal costume, minus the tail.

"Is something wrong?" Eve asked me, as I dished out chocolate fudge for her, strawberry for me.

"Nothing really," I said. "What made you ask?"

"You just seemed kind of . . . I don't know," said Eve. "You weren't laughing at the movie."

"It wasn't all that funny."

"Some of it was funny."

"I guess," I said.

We sat on stools at the kitchen island. The counter-top was a huge slab of black granite, so shiny it looked like the surface of a dark lake. It was cold against my bare forearms. I had liked the old blue Formica counters better, before my mom had the kitchen all gutted and redone. The old kitchen had been smaller, with a pantry and dinette on one side. My mom had wanted one "big open space" as she called it, even though she'd always left the cooking to our housekeeper. The new kitchen had a cavernous refrigerator, a restaurant-sized stove, and two separate sinks.

The strawberries in the ice cream were frozen hard as stones. I had to thaw them with my tongue against my teeth so they could be soft enough to chew.

"We're moving," I said.

"How come?" asked Eve. "This is a great apartment, and you've got such a great view."

"I know," I said.

"Where are you moving to?" Eve asked. Then she grinned. "Uptown? Closer to me?"

"I'm not sure," I said. Eve tilted her face, expectant. I looked down at my bowl and then back up at her. "Actually, we're moving out of the city, to the country, where my grandfather lives, when school's out."

Eve's spoon clattered on the granite. "But you're coming back, aren't you?" she asked.

"I think so," I said. "But nothing's very certain."

"That sucks," said Eve.

It was a word I'd never heard her use before.

"Yup," I said.

"Are your parents getting divorced?" she asked.

"No."

"Well, that's something," she said. She took the elastic off her ponytail, shook her hair out around her shoulders, then gathered it back into a new ponytail, while she held the elastic in her teeth. Her hair was pulled tight back off her face now, giving her a severe, pinched look.

I put the ice cream back in the freezer and set the bowls and spoons by the dishwasher. I was afraid of the next question Eve would ask. And she did ask it.

"Then how come you're moving?"

My mom had said we were just staying at my grandfather's while she found an apartment that was "better suited to our needs for right now." My dad had put it differently. "Your grandfather is taking us in, Irene," he told me, "because, at the moment, we're flat-out broke."

"I don't really know," I told Eve.

We went back to the living room and climbed back into our sleeping bags.

"Are you going to tell Frankie?" asked Eve.

Frankie was lying on her side now, one arm flung high above her head, as if she had been asking a question in class in a dream.

"You can if you want to," I said. "But I don't want anyone else at school to know."

"OK," said Eve. She was quiet then for so long I thought she had fallen asleep, but after a while, she whispered.

"Irene? Are you awake?"

"Yes," I whispered.

"You are coming back to our school, aren't you?"

"I suppose."

"You have to!" cried out Eve. "How could you not come back? Think about us! Think about RM!"

RM was what we called Mr. McClure. Eve and Frankie knew how I felt about him. The thought of him now—his face tilted to show concern—made me wince.

"I might not be able to, if we're still living in the country."

"Then you can stay with me," she said. "If your parents would let you. I know my parents wouldn't mind. You could live with us during the week and then live with your parents in the country on the weekends."

"Thanks," I said.

"I mean it."

"I know," I said. "Thank you."

I knew that Eve was trying to be nice, but she didn't really understand what was happening. I couldn't blame her for that—I didn't really understand it myself—but I felt irritated with her anyway. She and Frankie were still my best friends, but things were different now. It didn't seem fair that they could go on having the lives that they always had and I had to give up everything in mine.

I turned on my back and pretended I was going to sleep. But I didn't even close my eyes for a while. I stared up at the window. There was a tiny blinking red spot making its way across the black sky. A tiny, brave plane of some kind, with unknown people inside—maybe a girl my age, a girl headed somewhere. A girl going someplace in the night, or someplace, maybe, a morning away.

chapter seven

It was a Tuesday morning when we left the city.
My dad's Jaguar, a burgundy so shiny you wanted to lick
it, had been sold, so he'd rented a car. My dad was going
to come back with my grandfather's truck to pick up
everything that wasn't going into storage.

The rented car was tan inside and out, bland and anon-
ymous, which was just fine with me. I didn't want to be
seen leaving the city; I wanted to be invisible. School
wasn't over yet, but my summer vacation had started a
week earlier. Most of my friends were away—at camp or
in Europe or Nantucket—but there was always a chance
someone I knew might still be around. In front of the
Italian restaurant we always went to, a waiter in a white
apron was sweeping the sidewalk and singing. I ducked
down so he wouldn't see me.

On the whole drive up to my grandfather's house, my parents barely spoke. My dad turned on the radio but my mom said it gave her a headache, so he turned it off. Then he hummed, but my mom said that gave her a headache too, so he stopped humming. I always used to love the drive to my grandfather's: the highway right along the Hudson, the river lapping along the edge of Manhattan, the bridge at the northern tip so high up it seemed like a splinter in the sky, the sense of the city being left far behind as we finally got into the greenness beyond. But that Tuesday morning, every familiar sight that we passed seemed different, as if I was leaving it behind forever, and when we finally got off the highway and turned onto my grandfather's road, the city seemed as far away as a distant nation, and I felt I had been exiled from my life.

My grandfather's house was close to the road, with fields and woods behind it. The place had been a farm once. Now my grandfather had a plant nursery—he supplied local garden stores—and only the fields closest to the greenhouse were really used. It was a small, white house, set on a hillside so it was two stories on one side, one on the other. I'd always liked my grandfather's house—it was comfortable and cozy—but it was different now. Now I was going to have to live here. The house looked as if it had shrunken since we'd last visited—how was it ever going to hold us all?—and the land around it seemed as if it had stretched, making the house seem even smaller, more alone.

My grandfather helped us unpack the car. He carried my parents' suitcases into the master bedroom. My dad didn't want my grandfather to give it up to them, but my grandfather said he preferred the room downstairs.

"It has a door straight outside, so I can come in and out as I please," he said. "I'll use the basement bathroom and leave the upstairs one to you."

My mom looked around the room as if trying to decide whether she would spend the night in it or not.

"Feel free to move things around any way you like," my grandfather said.

"Thank you, Arthur," she said. I knew that my mom didn't like my grandfather very much, but she made it a point to always be polite.

My grandfather had put a vase of flowers on the dresser in my small bedroom and pulled the curtains open wide so the room felt full of light. On the nightstand beside the plain maple bed, my dad's when he was a boy, there was a painted china lamp.

"I don't remember that being here," I said.

"Found it in the attic," my grandfather said. "It was your grandmother's. Thought if you were reading in bed at night you might not want to get up to turn off the switch to the overhead when you go to sleep."

I was named Irene, after my grandmother, but she'd died before I was old enough to know her. My mom said she always expected that my grandfather would find himself another wife to look after him, but he never did.

He'd always lived alone, for as long as I could remember, looking after himself.

"Thank you for the lamp," I said.

"Got some lunch for you folks out in back," my grandfather said.

On the picnic table behind the house he had laid out an elaborate assortment of cold cuts, obviously an attempt to please us all. Usually when we visited, my mom brought food from the deli in the city—she didn't believe there was a decent delicatessen outside of New York—but she hadn't brought anything this time. A net umbrella had been set up to keep insects off the meats and cheese. Bees and butterflies made out of pipe cleaners clung to the green netting. My mom ate a little, then excused herself and said she needed to go lie down for a while. My dad picked at a slice of salami, a slice of turkey, then slowly began to warm to eating. He sat down beside my grandfather, who had made himself a large sandwich, and made an even larger one, and they seemed so comfortable there, these two gangly men, chewing in the sunshine, you'd think that nothing out of the ordinary had happened, that nothing had gone wrong in our lives. Between them they polished off all the roast beef, all the Swiss cheese, and all the pickles, and the bowl full of olives was reduced to two small piles of pits.

chapter eight

When I came into the kitchen in the morning, my grandfather was making orange juice. The sliced-open orange was bright as the sun outside the kitchen window. He pressed it down against the grooves of the green glass juicer, his hand pushing hard and twisting till the orange half was just a shell. He poured the juice into a glass for me.

"Where's Dad?" I asked.

"He was up early. He's out in the greenhouse. Your mother's not up yet."

"I know," I said.

The juice was sweet. Nothing like the juice we always had at home that said "fresh squeezed," but smelled of its waxed paper container and had no sweetness left in it at all.

"Sleep all right?"

I nodded.

"How're you doing?"

"OK, I guess."

But—surprisingly—it was better than OK, for the moment. Just my grandfather and me and the kitchen, filling with sunlight, and Joppy, my grandfather's dog, one blue eye, one brown, his tail thumping on the floor. Dogs he'll have, but not cats, though he's admitted cats are the only way to keep the mice down.

"No cats," I remember him saying. "Never liked them. Never will."

My grandfather looks like my dad. They are both tall with long arms and long necks and long noses and kind blue-green eyes. My grandmother must have had the mildest set of genes, for they barely touched the surface of my dad's face.

My grandfather set a bowl on the table and two new boxes of cereal.

"Your choice," he said.

One was Cheerios, which he'd always had when we came to visit, the other some sugary cereal that I knew he had bought for my benefit. He watched my face as I examined the box. He smiled and shrugged. "What do I know?" he asked. "Maybe your mother will like it."

This made us both laugh—my mom, whose idea of breakfast was a cup of coffee, black, and on special occasions, a half a bagel without anything on it.

My grandfather held his finger to his lips and pointed with his chin at the bedroom door. "Finish up," he said. "I have something to show you out in the barn.

❉ ❉ ❉

My grandfather's house had been built when my dad was a boy, but the barn had been built a hundred years before that. The barn boards were the same rough brown as the trunks of the tree beside it, and the foundation was built out of stones that had been cleared from the fields. The house looked like an intruder on the landscape, but the barn looked as if it had grown right out of the ground itself.

In the front section of the barn, my grandfather stored his tractors, tools, and greenhouse supplies. The back of the barn was a museum of outdated equipment and furniture—neatly arranged, because my grandfather was a tidy pack rat—scythes and apple baskets, a wringer-washer and an assortment of chairs with a variety of ailments. My dad's old sled and his cross-country skis were near the door, where they'd been for years, ready and hopeful each time it snowed.

"Check out the hayloft," my grandfather said.

When I was little I would play house up in the hayloft. My grandfather had rigged up a knotted rope, so I could swing down. I still liked to climb up to the hayloft when we visited, but I hadn't spent time up there in years.

My grandfather followed me up the wooden ladder. The hayloft had been swept clean. An old velvet loveseat with paw feet had been placed by the small window, with two old lawn chairs arranged across from it. Wooden pear boxes had been stacked as a bookcase, and a table had been fashioned out of an old pallet and boards.

"Thought you might want a place you could come to—you always liked it up here—and figured you were too old for camping out in the hay."

"It's wonderful, Grandpa. Thank you," I said.

I sat on the loveseat. Tufts of batting poked out from the crevice where the armrests met the seat, and the upholstery stitching had given out across the front, but the gold velvet still had its sheen.

"How did you ever get this up here?" I asked.

"A little luck," said my grandfather. "And a lot of help."

Beside the loveseat was a wrought-iron standing lamp with a parchment shade.

"Got a heavy duty extension cord up here," my grandfather said. "Switch is down by the barn door. You'll have to be careful and remember to turn it off every time you leave."

"I will," I said.

My grandfather sat on one of the lawn chairs across from me. He put his feet up, cautiously, on the table, tested the table top's balance, seemed satisfied with his work.

"You can have your friends up here," my grandfather said. "Hang out. Whatever they call it now."

The morning sunlight had rounded the corner of the barn and was straining across the window, illuminating a perfect spider web that had been invisible before.

"I don't have any friends here," I said. "All my friends are back in New York."

My grandfather let his breath out slowly. "Of course," he said. "I'm sorry about that, Irene."

"It's not your fault, Grandpa."

"Not anyone's fault, really," he said.

"I don't know about that," I said quickly.

"Your father's been doing his best to find another job," he said.

"I didn't mean Daddy."

"Oh," my grandfather said. He lifted his head and lowered it slowly. We sat there for a while, without saying anything.

"Funny thing about blame, Irene," he said. "It may make you feel a little better at first but it doesn't seem to do much to make you feel better in the long run."

"Maybe," I said.

chapter nine

After dinner I went out to work in the greenhouse with my grandfather. The greenhouse was warm and brightly lit and had a moist, rich smell that was part plant and part soil. Everything was orderly and predictable and patient. The plants were all lined up in perfect rows. The new green plastic pots were stacked up at the end of the table. Beside it, there was a pile of potting soil, the vermiculite twinkling as if it was bits of raw jewels.

My grandfather gave me a stack of white plant labels. *Dicentera exceliblis*, *bleeding heart*, they said. It was my job to stick one into the soil beside each small potted plant. My grandfather and I didn't talk; he was intent on his business. The fans whirred a steady, pleasant drone. When I was done, the table before me looked like a miniature graveyard.

"What should I do next?" I asked.

"You can help make up some pots with me, if you'd like."

"Sure," I said.

"You might want to go put on an old shirt first, if you have one. Or grab an apron from the back of the kitchen door."

I was about to say, "It doesn't matter," but I looked down at my T-shirt. It was white, and remarkably I hadn't gotten any dirt on it yet. It wasn't a shirt I really cared about, but I didn't want to run the risk that my mom would make an issue over it.

"OK," I said. "I'll be right back."

I went quietly into the house through the back door, and stopped in the kitchen to get a drink of water. My parents were in their bedroom, arguing. I had just reached for the faucet, but I didn't turn the water on.

"But she can't spend the summer just hanging around!" my mom was saying.

"There's simply no money right now for tennis camp. You know that, Andie."

"But she needs to do something productive this summer. And I don't mean working here, on this place. I'm not raising my daughter to be a farmer."

"No one suggested anything like that," said my dad.

"There must be some sort of recreation program in this town—swimming or summer school or—"

"Maybe she could use some time without any scheduled activities. Her life during the school year has always seemed pretty relentless to me, one activity after another.

She's still a kid, Andie. Maybe she needs some time to just goof off."

"Goof off. That's what you want for your daughter?" My mom's voice had risen to a shriek.

My dad stepped out into the hallway. The door slammed behind him. My dad stood in the silence afterward. He did not notice me in the dark of the kitchen. I crept out quietly, grabbing an apron, which luckily seemed to be waiting there for me, from behind the kitchen door. I ran out to the greenhouse.

My grandfather showed me how to fill the bottom of each pot, set the plant in, fill the soil in around it. We worked side by side.

"Something on your mind?" he asked me after a while.

I shrugged.

"Hey," he said, "you're not supposed to be back at the house now, are you?"

"No," I said.

"Don't worry about your mother," my grandfather said. "She'll settle in after a while."

"I don't think she ever will," I said. "She hates being here."

"And you, Irene, do you hate being here too?"

"No, not really."

My grandfather put down his trowel, wiped his hands off on his pants, and put his arms around me.

"I know it's what you miss that's the problem," he said. "But I have a feeling things will take a turn for the better."

"You think Daddy's going to get another job soon?"

"I don't know about that," said my grandfather. "No—what I was talking about wasn't anything to do with him. It's more a feeling I have about you."

My grandfather kissed the top of my head, then turned back to the table. "How about we set up a little production line here? One of us scoops and the other of us plants, and we move the pots right along, from one end to the other."

"All right," I said.

I hadn't known it, but I guess I'd been longing to plunge my hands into that mound of dark brown soil. Now I dug deep into it, buried my arms up to my elbows. I could imagine letting my whole body sink forward into it, pressing my face into the soil.

"I could use some pots now," my grandfather said.

I filled the two I had lined up, and passed them along to him. Then I filled two more. I kept filling and passing. I liked the feel of the soil on my fingers, the smell of the soil and the plants. After a while I was able to let it take me over; I was able to not think about anything else. I let the task I was doing be everything I was.

chapter ten

I brought a box of my things out to the loft and started arranging everything on the bookcase my grandfather had made of stacked-up pear boxes. On one shelf I lined up the books I'd brought with me. On another I placed my notebooks and stationery and the plastic cube of drawers that I'd packed with little things from my desk at home: pens, markers, stickers, paper clips, my collection of erasers. Strangely, they looked as if they belonged there.

The barn was quiet and had a sweet, comforting smell. There were no animals living in it, but once cows and sheep and a horse or two had made their home here, and I liked to imagine them here still, chewing and grunting and flicking their tails. Now all that lived here were mice and spiders and swallows, whose mud nests were pasted to the rafters.

There was no Internet here at my grandfather's, but that was OK for now. Frankie was already at the camp in Maine she had gone to every summer of her life—she was a junior counselor this year—and Eve was heading off to her family's place on Nantucket. Neither of them would be online, so we were stuck with letters anyway. I didn't mind. I liked writing by hand on nice paper; it was more like drawing a picture. In the barn, in the soft light, it felt effortless to cover page after page. All week long I wrote letters to Eve and Frankie and my other friends back home—letters that I sent, and letters that I didn't. The letters that I sent talked about my grandfather's farm as if it was a place we had come to for vacation. That was the way it was easy to think about everything. It was vacation time, after all, and soon no one I knew would be left at home in the city. The letters that I sent never said anything about why we had left or that I didn't know if I was coming back.

The letters that I didn't send told them everything, even the things that were the worst, like my mom standing in front of her bedroom closet a month before, pulling dresses down off their hangers and throwing them back at my dad, shouting, "Take this, and this one too. Take them all. I know you begrudge me every one." And my dad reaching to touch her shoulder and then withdrawing his hand.

At the end of the week, my grandfather surprised me with a bike that he had bought for me at a tag sale. It was a racing bike, white, in OK shape. If I was going to get a bike at all, I would have wanted a mountain bike, but my grandfather was clearly so pleased with having found this one for me, I had to pretend it was what I would have wanted. He adjusted the seat and handlebars for me and greased the chain. There was a bell mounted on the handlebars, with a medal on it.

"What's this?" I asked.

My grandfather put on his glasses and took a closer look. "It's a St. Christopher medal," he said. "St. Christopher is the patron saint of travelers. The bike must have belonged to someone Catholic. Do you want me to take it off for you?"

"No, it's OK," I said.

"Well, it won't hurt you," my grandfather said, laughing.

I touched the raised surface on the bell. Whoever the girl was who owned the bike before me had kept the medal shiny, even though the rest of the bike wasn't especially clean.

When I told my parents about the bike at dinner my mom looked over at my grandfather.

"I trust you bought her a helmet to go along with it."

My grandfather didn't miss a beat. "We're planning to go into town tomorrow to get her one," he said.

My mom turned back to me. "You're not allowed on that bike until you have a proper helmet," she said.

"Mom—" I began, but my dad interrupted.

"Think you've got my old bike somewhere in the back of that barn?" my dad asked my grandfather.

"Wouldn't have thrown it out," said my grandfather.

"I'll have to unearth it and get it cleaned up. Then we could go riding together sometime, Irene. I could use the exercise."

"You never used that exercise bike I bought you in the city," my mom said.

"Never made sense to me," my dad said. "If I'm going to put a lot of energy into pedaling I want to get someplace farther than the room I started out in."

My grandfather drove me to the bicycle shop in town the next day. He bought me a helmet, a rearview mirror, a water bottle holder, and a neat little pouch that hooked onto the handlebars with Velcro straps. I went riding that afternoon and every day after that, all week.

This was entirely different from riding on the bike path in Central Park. I'd never been allowed to ride on my own before, never been able to go wherever I wanted and explore places I'd never been. I'd never flown down a hill so fast it took my breath away.

On Sunday morning my dad decided he wanted to join me. He did manage to find his old bicycle in the archives of the barn, but the tires were both flat and the chain was all rusted. He propped the bike near the barn door, saying he'd work on it later in the week, but I think neither of us believed he ever really would.

chapter eleven

The day I met them all, my dad had gone into the city by train, but my mom had stayed behind. I wanted to get out of the house before she was up, so I had breakfast with my grandfather, and then I set off on my bike. My grandfather was out in the field beyond the greenhouse. I clanged the bell a few times and he looked back and waved at me. I pedaled fast down the dirt driveway, swerving to avoid the now-familiar ruts and rocks. One rock was shaped so much like the back of a turtle that it nearly fooled me every time.

I bicycled along the curving, narrow road toward the bridge over the parkway. It was a stone bridge, the kind that you would expect to be crossing a river, but instead of water, four lanes of cars flowed underneath. When my grandfather bought the farm, there was no parkway at all.

It was built when my dad was boy, and he'd played with his toy trucks there in the late afternoon, after the construction crews had gone home. My grandfather showed me a photograph from then: my dad, a little boy in overalls, pushing a yellow dump truck over a giant sand pile, the sunset settling into the valley around him.

When you crossed the highway you were in another town. The road changed its name and became straight and wide, with a sidewalk along one side. The giant slates were uneven and tilted from time and maple roots. I liked to ride along the sidewalk, my bicycle bumping up and down over the angles of the stones.

The houses were set along both sides of the road, close enough so they could see their neighbors. Some of the houses were Colonial style and stately; some were Victorian, with cupolas and porches; some were smaller modern houses tucked in between them. One was a stone mansion, with lots of gables and three immense chimneys. It was a gloomy house, the kind you would imagine was inhabited by ghosts, but instead it was inhabited by a family with many kids. I knew this because the lawn in front was worn to dirt, and there were always bikes lying in the driveway and toys and gear flung on the front steps. And because I'd seen the family when I'd ridden by, I'd spotted a girl my age—and a number of other kids.

Every day I rode by the stone house I'd try to catch more glimpses of the kids who lived there, yet if there was any chance that I would be noticed, I'd pedal fast and keep my eyes straight ahead, for fear of being caught watching. If they saw me I wanted them to think I was on my way somewhere, that I wasn't just a girl on a bike with nothing to do and no place to go.

That morning I rode past the stone house, toward the street that led to town. It was a long steep hill into town, and I took it carefully, the brakes squealing, my hands sore from gripping them. I rode out past the library to the War Memorial, along the river. I took off my helmet and hung it from the handlebars, where it clunked against the bike. I liked the feel of my hair blowing out behind me and the image I had of myself with my hair that way. I rang the bell once, just to hear its clear, bright sound.

At the War Memorial, there was a bandstand that no band played on and a row of benches that no one sat on. The pavement was smooth and nice to ride along. But I didn't ride on the stones around the monument in the center, because they were engraved with the names of all of the men and boys from town who had been killed in World War I, and then World War II and Korea, almost like graves. They had run out of room for Vietnam, and the names of those who died there were listed on a separate slab of stone, the color of raw steak, which was set upright among the ivy along the riverbank.

It was getting hotter when I started back toward home, and I had to walk the bike up the hill. It was longer and steeper than it seemed coming down. When I reached the top my heart was pounding so hard it seemed like a small animal trying to escape from my chest. I laid my bike against the embankment of someone's lawn and took a drink from my water bottle. The water was warm and had a smell of plastic.

I rode back along Deerborn Street along the sidewalk, looking down at the paving stones, bumping my bike up and down over the edges. When I got near the stone house, I saw a group of kids on the front lawn playing soccer. It was already too late to switch over to the other side of the street; I didn't want to do anything to call attention to myself. A lawn chair had been set up at each end of the lawn to act as a goalpost, and a blond boy, around my age, was about to take a goal kick. My shoelace had become loose, and I used this as an excuse to stop. I bent to tie it, protected enough, I thought, from the players' sight by some bushes.

But the ball, as if I had willed it, departed from the boy's foot, selected an unlikely path through the air, headed directly my way, and landed with certainty in the exact spot between the front wheel of my bike and my shoe.

chapter twelve

I propped my bike on its kickstand and picked up the ball. The kids on the lawn were all looking at me, waiting. For a moment everything was still, quiet. The only thing that was certain was the feel of the ball against my palms. I looked down at the surface of it, hexagons of black and white all fitting perfectly together. I did not move.

Then, it was as if a spell had been broken, and I threw the ball back toward the group of kids. The boy who had kicked the ball stopped it neatly with his chest, then trapped it with his foot. "Hey, do you play soccer?" he shouted at me.

I had played soccer in gym at school, but I wasn't very good at it. I wasn't good at any sports.

"Not really," I said.

"Would you join us anyway?" the boy asked. "We're short a player on one team."

"I guess so," I said.

"Great!" he said.

I moved my bike to the side of the pavement and walked toward the group of kids. The boy walked toward me. He wasn't any taller than I was, but he was older than I had first thought, maybe a couple of years older than me. He had a smile on his face that was so welcoming, so easy to smile back at, that I did.

"I'm Jim," he said. He held out his hand. I'd never seen a kid do this before, but I extended my hand and he shook it. He turned back toward the group on the lawn and pointed: "Our neighbors, Phil and Rachel, and us, Meg, Stover, Lolly, Theo, Bloomer..." The last, I gathered, was the dog, who looked up at the sound of his name and cocked his head.

"And you?" Jim asked.

"Irene," I said.

"As in that old song 'Goodnight Irene'?"

I smiled. My dad used to sing that to me every night when I was little. "Well, not from the song, but—"

"How old are you?" he asked.

"Thirteen."

"Meg just turned fourteen," he said, pointing to the tall girl in the group. "You moved here recently?"

"We're visiting my grandfather."

"He's got the greenhouse, right?"

"How'd you know?"

"Figured. You came from out that way. And I know the place. I've worked there."

I didn't ask how he knew where I came from. This implied he'd been watching me. I wasn't sure what to say next.

"Jim, come on! Let's play." One of the little boys was yelling now.

"Right," said Jim. He put his hand on my shoulder and steered me to the kids. "This is Irene," he said. "Irene, you'll be with Meg. Stover, you're with me now." Jim set the ball on the ground in front of me. "Try a practice kick," he said.

I stood behind the ball and got ready to kick.

"Not with your toe, though," Jim said. "Use the side of your foot."

I steadied myself and kicked. And with that brief introduction I found myself playing soccer, and I was transformed from a girl alone on a bike, who had no place to go, to a girl who had been adopted as a member of a team.

They were all good at soccer—even the littlest one—but especially the girl named Meg, who was fast and graceful, and Jim, who seemed to be everywhere at once, dashing for the ball, bouncing it off his head, his chest, leaping as high as I could imagine anyone could leap, and cheering on both teams simultaneously. The younger sister Lolly, was one of the thinnest girls I'd ever seen, and though she stood gasping for breath after bouts of running (something which no one seemed to notice) she played with fierce determination.

I was quite hopeless, but they didn't seem to think so, or at least they were all unusually generous. After the game Jim slung his arm over my shoulder and said, "Good game."

I'd never had a boy do this to me before, put his arm around me in such an easy, friendly way, but I knew it meant nothing in particular. Jim was clearly someone who made physical contact with everything—he tousled his little brother's hair; he hugged his sister Lolly when she made a goal; he embraced the dog.

"Let's go in and get something to drink," said Jim. And so everyone trooped inside, and I moved along with them, caught in the movement, in the sense of camaraderie, which had happened so quickly, so miraculously, that I hardly dared believe it could last for very long.

chapter thirteen

There were five of them. Jim was the oldest and obviously the leader. He was a year older than Meg, but she was a lot taller, and from a distance you might think she was the older of the two. She walked as if she were apologetic about her height. Meg was really pretty, but she didn't act like someone who thought she was, and she was really shy. Her little sister, Lolly, would have been pretty too, except she was so thin that's all you could think of when you looked at her. No one in the family looked alike, and I wondered if they all had the same two parents. They all had different combinations of hair and eye color—from Jim, who was blond and blue eyed, to Lolly who had brown hair and eyes so dark they looked black. I thought of a doll catalog I once had where there were eight different choices of eye color and twenty different choices of hair color, and I got to pick the doll that looked most like me.

Jim led everyone—including the neighbors who'd been playing with us—through the house to the kitchen. He got out the lemonade, Meg got out the paper cups, and drinks were poured and served. It seemed as if they did this every day.

It was an enormous kitchen, with old-fashioned cabinets—not the kind made to look old, but ones that really were. The stove was new, but an antique one still stood against the wall, covered with houseplants. There was a battered sofa and a big, round table surrounded by an assortment of chairs. I'd never seen a sofa in a kitchen before.

"Would you like a house tour?" Jim asked.

"Sure," I said.

"Everyone does," said Jim.

Meg and the other kids followed along behind us. They seemed to follow Jim wherever he went—or were they just curious about me? Jim sounded like he had given this tour a lot of times before. "The guy who built this house owned a lumber business," he said. "And every room is paneled in a different kind of wood." He pointed to a brass fixture on the wall. "Gas lamps," he said. "When they added electricity, they left those in too."

There were a lot of kids in this family, but the house was so big it could have easily absorbed another dozen without seeming full. There was an enormous living room, a library, a billiard room, a sunroom, and a dining room the size of a banquet hall. I thought of my grandfather's house and the way there was no place to go to get away from anyone.

What was odd, though, was the way the house was decorated—or rather the way it wasn't decorated. It was a mansion, but the furniture was shabby and there wasn't quite enough of it to go around. Everywhere I noticed things that would have made my mom wince. Kids' paintings were taped right up on the walls; clothing was draped over the banister of the grand staircase; and the massive stone fireplace in the front hall was used to store boots.

A coat of arms hung over the mantelpiece. The shield said *"Vulpes"* and in gold letters across the bottom: *"Semper ludibundus."*

I knew "semper" from Latin class. "Always ludibundus?" I asked.

"Playful," said Jim. "Our name is Fox, Vulpes in Latin, but we don't have a coat of arms—my dad's family is Greek. A friend of his made it for him as a joke."

"Fox doesn't sound like a Greek name," I said.

"It's not. It's translated from the Greek. When my great-great-grandfather came to America he knew some English, so at Ellis Island, when they went to write down his name, he gave them the translation."

The rooms on the second floor were laid out in an odd, unpredictable way, with so many doorways and corridors I lost my bearings and was surprised when we ended up back in the center hall.

"Meg will show you her room upstairs. My dad's office is up there so we won't all go up. Meg can have a third-floor room because she's the only one he trusts to be quiet."

Meg looked at Jim as if pleading with him to come along too, but he was herding the other kids downstairs. I followed Meg upstairs. One corner of her room was a round turret. It had narrow, leaded-glass windows, and the walls were so thick that each window had a built-in window seat, just wide enough for one person to sit.

I kneeled on the window seat and looked out the window. At the end of the driveway my bike was propped against the stone wall. It seemed very little, very far away.

I looked back at the room. It was neater than most of the house. There was a futon on the floor, and a matching bureau and desk. The ceiling was high and mobiles hung from a string stretched from wall to wall. "I like that one," I said, pointing to a mobile with parrots that looked like miniature real birds.

Meg gave it a tap with her fingertip, and the parrots circled slowly, each one rotating on its little wire perch. We both watched them for a while.

"This is a great room," I said.

"Thanks," said Meg. She seemed so awkward I didn't know what to say next. I looked at the built-in bookcase along the wall. It had doors with leaded-glass panes. I tilted my head to look at the titles.

"Here," said Meg, and she swung the doors open. "They're arranged alphabetically by author."

I smiled. "Mine too," I said.

I looked over the books. I touched the spine of *The Catcher in the Rye*. "My friend Eve said I would like it," I said, "but I haven't read it yet. Have you?"

"I've read everything here. Most of them more than once. It's one of my favorites. Want to borrow it?"

Borrow, I thought instantly, that meant return too. I looked at Meg. Her face was eager, full of hope.

I slid the book from its shelf. "Sure," I said.

A boy with red hair, the one called Stover, came bursting into the room. "Mommy's back," he shouted. "Wanna go for a swim?"

"Shh," Meg whispered, and pointed down the hallway. "Daddy's working."

"Well, do you?" asked Stover again, in a voice only a little softer.

"Maybe," she said, and Stover dashed off.

"What does your dad do?" I asked.

"Computer stuff," she said, shrugging. "He works late at night and sleeps late in the morning, then works most of the day. Though he does come out for meals and other things. And really, he's very nice."

She seemed surprised at herself for saying so much. She was clearly not someone who generally talked a lot. "We have a pool out back. Would you like to go swimming?"

"I need to go home for lunch," I said. "And anyway, I'd need to get my bathing suit."

"Why don't you come back after lunch, then? I mean, if you want to," said Meg. "We'll be here. My mom doesn't let us use the pool unless she's home, but she'll be here all day."

I wanted to shout out, "Yes! I'll come, of course!," but I was afraid to sound too eager.

"OK," I said.

chapter fourteen

My mom thought it looked as if it might rain, so she decided we should eat lunch inside. She kept telling me not to let my grandfather do all the work, but although she fluttered around, she did nothing useful herself. My mom used to cook on occasion—special gourmet dinners when my parents had guests—but she had no patience with ordinary meals. When we didn't have our housekeeper anymore, she left the regular cooking to my dad, and she rarely helped with the cleaning up. Now, here at my grandfather's, my mom seemed content to leave all kitchen work to my grandfather or my dad. Her main contribution was suggesting that we go out to eat more, though there was no restaurant in town she liked.

While we were eating, my mom asked me about what I had been doing all morning. I didn't tell her that I had ridden to town, but I did tell her I'd met some kids. "They invited me over later for a swim," I said.

My grandfather seemed to know the house and the family.

"Who are these people?" my mom asked.

"Jim Fox, the oldest one, worked for me. An enterprising young man. Organized a group of younger kids to work under him. He was the contractor." My grandfather laughed.

"And the family?"

"Nice family," my grandfather said. "Lots of kids."

"Five," I said. "There's a girl my age."

"Five?" my mom said, and she gave a little shudder.

"Don't worry, Andrea," my grandfather said, smiling. "The father's designed some software that's probably worth millions, so they can more than feed their brood."

My mom settled back in her chair, with a look of relief. I wanted it not to matter to her what their father did. I wanted Meg to be acceptable to her not just because she thought Meg's family was well-off.

"See, it is raining," my mom said. "I was right about us eating indoors."

I looked out the window. She was right.

"Well, good for you," I said.

My mom looked at me with surprise, at first, then anger. "Irene!" she called, but I was already out the back door, running across the yard to the barn.

My loft had held on to the heat of the morning. It smelled of hay and cows and dust and time. I curled on my old velvet loveseat and listened to the rain, heavy now on the barn roof.

I thought I might want to read, but I realized I had never taken the book that Meg was going to lend me, and there was no book of my own that I wanted to open. I wondered what Meg was thinking when she saw the rain. I wondered if she would remember that she had asked me over, if she had noticed the book I'd left behind. I wondered what Meg's family would be doing when it rained.

I wondered if it was raining in the city. I didn't think my dad had brought an umbrella with him. I pictured him sitting at some important interview, pushing his wet hair back off his forehead, drying his glasses off on the inside of his cuff.

Maybe everything worked out for him today, and he got the kind of job he was looking for. We could go back home to the city. We could buy back our old penthouse and reclaim all our furniture from storage, and I could put all my posters back up on my walls and set up my brass canopy bed. And it wouldn't matter that I never went swimming at the Foxes and the book that Meg had wanted to lend me was lying, facedown, on the corner of her desk.

After a while, my grandfather came into the barn. He walked under the loft and called to me.

"Can I come up?" he asked.

"Sure," I said.

He took off his slicker, shook it out, and hung it on the back of a wheelbarrow handle. He climbed up the ladder to the loft and sat down on the aluminum chair across from me. When he put his feet up on the table, he noticed his boots, wet and dirty. He laughed, set his feet on the floor, and wiped off the table with the side of his hand.

"So," he said. "Looks like swimming is off for this afternoon. I can give you a ride over to your friend's, though, if you'd like."

"She didn't really invite me to just come over. It was for the swim," I said.

"Oh." We sat there for a while, then my grandfather said, "You could give her a ring and see what she's up to. People like visitors when it rains."

"I don't know her number," I said.

"I suppose I could dig it up for you."

"That's all right, Grandpa," I said. "I couldn't really just call her up. It's not that sort of thing."

"I see," my grandfather said. "Well, there was something I came to tell you anyway. I just want you to know that you can ask anyone you want over here anytime. And that pond out back. It's not great for swimming, but sometimes kids like to fish or just muck around in it. And I was thinking that someplace in this barn I've got an old canoe and maybe if you'd give me a hand we could drag it out and clean it up. Not sure it doesn't have holes in the bottom, but it's worth taking a look."

"You don't have to do all this for me, Grandpa," I said.

"It's nice to have your company around here, Irene," my grandfather said. "I never used to get to see you as much as I wanted to."

I thought about all the times my dad had wanted to go up to my grandfather's for a visit, but most weekends and in the summer my mom always had so many other plans. When my grandfather came into the city to visit us—for my recitals, school plays—he always seemed out of place in our apartment. My mom was quick to pluck up his jacket if he draped it over a chair, or wipe up the circle of moisture his glass left on the surface of a table.

"Are they really millionaires?" I asked.

My grandfather got a funny look on his face.

"Oh, dear, Irene, you've caught me there," he said. "I'm afraid that's not something I know as a fact, one way or the other. But I know Fox does something with software design, and from what I hear, most of those fellows are millionaires, so I didn't think it would hurt if your mom reached that conclusion."

"Oh, Grandpa!" I said.

chapter fifteen

I could tell that things hadn't gone well in the city that day. My mom had gone to pick up my dad at the railroad station, and it was a long time before they got back. I figured they had driven around for a while, to have a chance to talk in private. They were done talking about things by the time they returned to the house. My dad was rumpled and tired, and although I knew his suit had been made to order, it looked like he was wearing a jacket that had been handed down to him by someone else.

At dinner my mom kept introducing cheerful, irrelevant subjects, but no one rose to the discussion. By the time the meal was over the quiet had turned my mom silent too.

"I could use your help in the greenhouse tonight, Irene," my grandfather said.

"All right," I said.

I was barely out the door before my mom's voice rose in the kitchen.

"You had every right to expect something from Bruce!" she said. "After all, how did he get where he is in the first place?"

I couldn't hear my dad's comment, but I could hear my mom's response, her voice higher now. "Why are you defending him? Why are you always defending people, even when they treat you this way?"

In the greenhouse it was warm and bright. The fans made their even, predictable drone.

"These irises all need larger pots," my grandfather said. "Why don't you work over here."

I went over to the table and picked up the first plant. It was just a little sprig of green, not much more than a few blades of grass. I looked at the plant tag. *Iris kampheri alba.*

"These?" I asked.

My grandfather nodded. He turned the plant on its side, tapped on the side of the pot, and eased the plant out of its old container. He was right. There was a little bit of unpromising plant visible on the top, but underneath the soil line, there was a thick clump of roots.

I brought a stack of two-quart pots over to the pile of potting soil. I squeezed a fistful and let it fall softly from my hand. The soil was brown as chocolate, and moist. I filled the bottom of each pot, set each plant into its new quarters, and filled in around it with fresh soil. Then I stuck the plant tag in the new pot.

"What if Daddy never gets another job?" I asked.

"I don't think you have to worry about 'never,'" my grandfather said. "It might take a while. But 'never'—no."

"I wish Mom would just lay off," I said.

"Yes," said my grandfather, smiling a little. "We all do."

"You don't like her very much, do you?"

My grandfather took a while to answer. "Your mother has many fine qualities," he said at last. "I set my mind on those."

I took another stack of new pots and started on the next batch of irises.

"Do you think Daddy will leave her?"

My grandfather looked at me with genuine surprise. "Have you been worrying about that, along with everything else, Irene?"

I shrugged.

"Well, that's something you don't have to worry about. There's a 'never,' for sure, I can promise you."

It was reassuring to hear him say that, but disappointing, in a way too. Everything had fallen apart, everything I was used to. So why not have my parents get divorced— like so many of my friends' parents did—why not just have that be part of it too? If your parents got divorced it explained everything. If you had to move or live with relatives or leave your school, you could just say "my parents got divorced" and everyone would understand. But what had happened to me I couldn't really explain. How could I? I didn't understand it myself. Sure, my dad had lost his job—was "between jobs" as my mom insisted I say—but that didn't account for us having to sell our apartment, auction off our nicest things, and move in with my grandfather as if we had nothing of our own.

"It's the way they lived," Jenna had said. "They couldn't keep on that way."

But how had that happened? Was everything we had not really ours? And the life that we'd led, was none of it real?

chapter sixteen

My grandfather was delivering a load of plants to the retailer in town the next morning. He and my dad had gotten up early to get everything ready, and after I ate breakfast I helped them load the truck. My dad was wearing coveralls like my grandfather, and they looked so much alike, working side by side, anyone who watched them would know they were father and son.

"Do you need me to come along to unload?" my dad asked.

"I was planning on asking Irene," my grandfather said. "I was thinking you'd work on the wall today."

My dad smiled. "I was hoping you'd say that."

My grandfather turned to me. "What do you say?"

"Sure, I'll come," I said.

My dad had undertaken rebuilding the retaining wall alongside the greenhouse. He had approached the project with relish, dismantling the old wall, hammering neat pegs into the ground and stretching a string between them to keep his line straight. My mom came out to see what he was up to.

"If you don't wear gloves," she said, "your hands will look like a farmer's. And then what?"

"Then what" meant that my dad would never get a job. Vice presidents did not have farmers' hands.

"I like to feel the stones," my dad said. He held a flat slab out in front of him and rubbed his thumbs along the surface. He gave my mom a smile.

I thought my mom would smile back. But she didn't smile. She pulled her lips in tight against her teeth as if they would hold in place everything she wanted to say but had chosen not to. Then she went back into the house. I noticed that my grandfather was watching it all.

I climbed up into the truck beside my grandfather, and we headed toward town.

"Every time Daddy does anything around here, Mom gets all angry at him. It doesn't seem fair," I said. "Daddy seems really happy to be doing stuff."

"Scares your mother, seeing him happy like that," my grandfather said.

"I don't get it."

"She's afraid he'll like it all too much and end up like me, I guess," said my grandfather.

"What's wrong with ending up like you?" I asked.

My grandfather reached over and touched the back of my head. "Nothing, Irene, from my point of view. But your mother sees it differently. She sees a man who went to law school and never practiced law. Came out to the country instead and did nothing very ambitious with his life."

"You have a business, Grandpa."

"It's a little business. It makes its way now, but when your dad was young I often had to work extra jobs—carpentry, driving the school bus—to get us through. Even so, we liked the life, Irene. I like it still. But it's not a life your mother would want."

It was a cool, cloudy morning. Every stretch of the roadway that had taken me a while to cover by bike went by so quickly from the car window it was hard to believe it was the same landscape. It seemed as if it had been cut and spliced somehow. We were over the highway before I knew it, and on to Deerborn Street. My grandfather slowed down and pulled over by Meg's house.

"Why are you stopping?" I asked.

"I thought you might want to get out here and visit with your friends while I'm in town."

"Don't you need my help unloading the truck?"

"No, I'll have help there."

"Then why did you want me along?"

My grandfather didn't say anything.

"Oh," I said, catching on. "But Grandpa, I can't just go up there and ring their bell."

"Why not?" he asked.

I looked at the house. It seemed strangely quiet and still. "It doesn't look like anyone's up."

"I'm sure they're up," said my grandfather.

"It's still too early. Maybe later. But it's too early now."

"All right, then," said my grandfather. "We'll stop on the way back."

My grandfather supplied plants for Country Gardens, a nursery on the outskirts of town. I'd driven past it before, but never gone in. It had a storybook quality to it, a cottage with arbors and trellises, the plants arranged along pebbled paths. The gravel in the parking lot was deep, and the truck tires made a swooshing sound, as if we were driving through water.

"Oh, Arthur, you're here!"

The woman who came out to meet the truck looked young from a distance, but her hair, pulled up into a ponytail, was grey, and up close she looked closer to my grandfather's age. She was wearing shorts and work boots, but she had on a fresh blue shirt and dangling earrings. I had the feeling that she was about to embrace my grandfather, but noticing me, held herself back.

"Lucia, this is Irene," my grandfather said.

Lucia took both my hands in hers. "I'm so glad to meet you, at last," she said.

Though I guessed she'd been expecting my grandfather to arrive alone, she'd been quick to hide whatever disappointment she might have felt. She pulled up some green metal carts and we handed out the flats of plants.

"I'll restock later," she said. "Now we'll just unload these by the fence. What treasures did you bring me today, Arthur?"

"You asked for nepeta," said my grandfather, handing out a box of plants in two-quart pots. "Parnassica and blue beauty."

"Parnassica?"

"It's new, even bigger than six hills giant," said my grandfather. "You'll like it."

"I like everything your grandfather brings me," said Lucia.

We unloaded the truck remarkably quickly. Lucia may have been old, but she was strong, and easily hefted a box full of plants while I struggled under its weight.

"Here are your irises," my grandfather said. "Cristata vein mountain and Abbey's violet."

"Oh, and alba. Thank you, Arthur, for remembering the alba."

They could have been speaking a secret language between the two of them. My grandfather hopped down out of the truck, and wiped off his hands on his pants legs. I climbed down and stood beside him.

"I have some lemonade inside," said Lucia.

"Can't say no to that," my grandfather said.

Lucia held the door open for us. "Come in and look around," she told me.

Inside, the cottage was one large room, all a shop. There were garden tools for sale, planters, baskets, and seeds, as well as handmade papers and soap. There was nothing plastic in sight. On one side there was a workshop area for making wreaths and dried flower arrangements.

Bunches of drying flowers hung from the rafters, and everything smelled of lavender and roses.

"I thought you lived here," I said.

Lucia laughed. "What a charming idea! I wish I could, but this isn't properly winterized, and of course it's right near the road. Someone lived here once, though. This was a working farm a hundred years ago."

My grandfather poured himself a glass of lemonade, sat down, and tilted his chair back, like a man who felt at home. Lucia poured a glass for me and for herself.

"Did the loveseat work out in the loft all right?" Lucia asked.

I looked over at my grandfather.

"One of Lucia's castoffs," he said.

I turned to her. "Oh," I said. "It's great. I would have thanked you if I'd known."

"It's I who needs to thank you. I have an attic that is stuffed beyond imagining. I'm always eager for excuses to unload some of it. You must come to my house sometime and look over everything and see if there is anything else that you can make use of. Blueberry bread?" she asked, holding out a plate to me.

I took a small piece. "Your grandfather's favorite," she said, and indeed my grandfather ate two large pieces, then one more.

My grandfather had written out a list of the plants he'd delivered and they looked this over together and discussed what he'd be bringing the next time. It was more a discussion between friends than a business arrangement. I had the feeling my grandfather would grow whatever struck his fancy and Lucia would sell whatever he chose to bring to her.

When it was time to go, Lucia walked us to the truck. She stopped at an arbor and pointed to a vine that was climbing there.

"Look at your terniflora, Arthur. I think it's going to have a wonderful season."

"Looks healthy enough," said my grandfather.

Lucia turned to me. "This is my favorite plant," she said. "It's a kind of clematis that blooms very late—it's called sweet autumn clematis, in fact. It has small white flowers, like tiny stars, long after most everything in the garden is finished, when you're feeling sad about the season coming to an end." Lucia gave me a hug. "Come back again soon," she said.

I climbed into the truck and turned just in time to see her reach up and touch my grandfather's face.

"Well," he said, after we had headed off. "So."

"So," I said.

It was strange that my grandfather had this person who was in his life whom we had never seen, never heard about before. But then again, there was probably a lot about my grandfather's life that we didn't know about. It had been easy to imagine him just living on his own, with no connections in the outside world. It had never occurred to me that there might be a woman who was interested in my grandfather. It had never occurred to me that anyone would see him that way.

chapter seventeen

When we drove near Meg's house, my grandfather slowed the truck, then came to a stop.

"It's not early anymore," he said.

"What will I say?"

"You'll say, 'Hi, I forgot to take the book you were going to lend me.'"

"I can't—"

My grandfather reached over and opened my door. "I'll sit here for a while in case you want to come home with me. Otherwise, stay as long as you like. Give me a call, and I'll pick you up later."

I got out of the truck and closed the door behind me. It didn't catch, so I had to open it and slam it hard. It was a loud noise. The only noise on the street. I walked up the front walkway and up on the porch. The screen door was closed, but the door was open behind it. I looked around for the doorbell, but couldn't find it. There was a door knocker on the inner door, but I didn't want to just open the screen door and step in. I tapped lightly on the door frame. Suddenly Lolly appeared in the hallway.

"Hi," she said. Then she yelled up the stairway behind her, "Meg, your friend is here."

She didn't open the screen door and invite me in, so I just stood there. I looked across the street. I couldn't exactly see my grandfather's face in the truck, but I knew he was watching me. I waited on the front porch, wondering what to do next.

After a minute, someone came down the stairs and opened the screen door—a woman with reddish curly hair that had been pinned up on top of her head, but spilled out all around her face. She reminded me of a princess in a children's book. She looked at me, her face a question.

"I'm waiting for Meg," I said.

"Did anyone tell her you're here?" Her voice was a young girl's voice, soft and musical.

"Lolly called her."

"In this house," she said, smiling, "you need to go and fetch people in person. No one hears anyone call them." She drew me into the front hall. I turned to look at my grandfather across the street. His truck was starting up.

"I'm Julie," said the woman. "Meg's mother. You must be Irene."

I nodded. I'd never seen anyone's mother who was

quite so beautiful. And she was wearing the kind of baggy T-shirt my mother would never wear, and no makeup.

"Why don't you just go upstairs. I know she's eager to see you."

I hesitated at the bottom of the stairs.

"It's just up and up," said Julie, twirling her finger, "then first door on the left."

I waited just a moment. There were feet on the stairs, coming down. It was Jim.

"Hi, Irene," he said. "Actually what I should say is 'Good day, Irene.'" He was smiling. "Looking for Meg, I bet."

I nodded.

"Come on," he said, and he tugged playfully at my sleeve.

He started sprinting up the stairs, but realized I wasn't quite up to his pace and stopped at the second floor landing to let me catch my breath.

"We do this up and down all the time," he said. "We're used to it." Meg's door was open partway. He knocked and pushed it fully open.

"I've brought you someone," he said, and it was only then that he let go of my hand.

Meg had been reading. She looked up, surprised, and for a second I was afraid I had intruded where I was not wanted, but her face changed quickly into a smile that was so full of pleasure, so open, that I knew instantly I had been wrong.

"Have fun, guys," said Jim.

He was turning to leave before I found my voice. "Hey, thanks," I said.

"See ya," he said, and he was gone.

I turned back toward Meg. She smiled and I smiled, but neither of us seemed to know how to begin a conversation. Finally I said, "I forgot to take the book."

"I know," said Meg. "I was hoping you'd come over, even though it was raining. I thought I'd call you, but I'm not very good at calling people."

"I thought I'd call you, but I'm not very good at calling people, either," I said.

Meg laughed, and I laughed. And although it wasn't very funny, we kept laughing and when either of us stopped, the other's laughter started us up again. I don't know what we were laughing about, really, but for us it was the way we became friends, laughing that way, laughing about nothing. And it was wonderful to just laugh like that, the first time I had laughed like that in days, in weeks. The first time I had laughed like that since everything had started going wrong in my life.

chapter eighteen

There are some friendships that you make slowly, building them up little by little, like laying bricks. And there are other friendships that you enter quickly and fully, like stepping into a finished house and feeling, "I'm home." I think that Meg and I became close so quickly because we both had recently been separated from our best friends. We both lucked out because of each other's losses.

Meg's best friend had lived across the street. Meg pointed out the house from her window. It was grey stucco with pointy gables, a house that looked pinched and vertical, with precisely trimmed shrubs across the front.

"Her father got some job as a screenwriter in L.A., and they moved in March. They live in a fancy house in Pasadena."

"That's nice," I said.

"She hates it," said Meg. "She hates her school. She wishes she could move back here. But I don't think her parents ever will."

We were making beaded bracelets on elastic thread. I'd offered to pay Meg back for the beads, but she said she had more than she could ever use, and though I tried to select the less expensive beads, she kept pushing the nicer ones my way.

"I've never been very good at making friends," said Meg. "They tend to be the people I already know, because they live nearby. Or they turn up somehow—"

"Like me," I said.

"You're just visiting here for the summer, aren't you?"

I nodded.

Just visiting for the summer. That was the only way I had been able to think about it. I hadn't told Meg why we were really here. She probably thought it was because we wanted to spend time with my grandfather. I hadn't said anything about selling our apartment or putting our things in storage. I hadn't told her that when my father went into the city he wasn't working, he was looking for a job, and that when my mom went into the city she was looking for an apartment we could afford.

Meg assumed, and I'd never said otherwise, that our old apartment was there, untouched, waiting for us when we went back in the fall. I didn't lie to her—I wouldn't lie to her—but I let her think that. I let her think that because I liked to think it too. I liked to imagine that everything of my old life was there, just on hold for the moment.

I take the elevator up to the top floor and open the door of our apartment. On the side table in the front hall, the day's mail is waiting in the china bowl with the clipper ships on it. I look through and see if there is anything for me. Then I run down the hall to the kitchen, grab a yogurt from the refrigerator, and head to my bedroom. Everything is just as I'd left it: the Beatles poster on my closet door; the dream catcher I'd made in 6th grade hanging from the frame of my canopy bed; the canisters of markers and pens lined up on my desk; the Christmas tree lights that I had tacked up along the molding; the big striped chair filled with stuffed animals by the window; and outside the window, flowers in the planters on the terrace; and beyond, the city, all out there, a million tiny windows, a million tiny lives.

✴ ✴ ✴

I went over to Meg's house every day that first week. We swam in their pool, played soccer, softball, volleyball, badminton, Ping-Pong, and what they called "all-terrain" croquet, which meant there was no croquet lawn, they just set up the wickets in the rough side yard of the house. It was like an informal day camp, and all the kids in the family and all the kids in the neighborhood who wandered by joined in. I'd never been in a group before where older kids and little kids, boys and girls, hung out with each other this way.

Jim was the best at whatever we did, but Meg was nearly as good. She was a lot better than their neighbor, Phil, who was Jim's age. When she and Jim played Ping-Pong the little ball moved so fast my eye couldn't follow it. I was a decent swimmer, but not very good at anything else. No one seemed to mind. And I didn't mind, because Jim took on the role of my coach, just as he'd done that first day when I'd met them all playing soccer. He adjusted my grip on the Ping-Pong paddle; he held a birdie in the air and had me practice serving for badminton; he guided the swing of my croquet mallet. When my croquet ball miraculously got through a wicket on one try, he whooped and clapped me on the back. I stood there, stupidly happy, and didn't realize when my turn came again until everyone started yelling at me.

Meg and I were alone when I first went swimming there, and when Jim turned up later I was already in the pool, and my body was safely hidden underwater. Meg and I were floating, holding on to a rubber raft. Jim dove into the pool and came up beside us.

"Hiya, Meggy," he said. "Good day, Irene." He pushed his wet hair back so it was off his face, then rested his head on his folded arms on the raft. We drifted, in perfect laziness. The water was just the ideal degree of cool, the sun on my shoulders was just the ideal warm. I could hear the younger kids' voices, off and on, in the distance. Then they must have gone inside, because it was so quiet all I could hear was the gentle sound of water from the dolphin-shaped fountain at the end of the pool. There was nowhere else on earth I wanted to be. No one else I wanted to be with. I wanted it to last and last, just this way.

Meg's mom came out of the house, surrounded by a bunch of kids. She had ice cream sandwiches for all of us. I got out of the pool with Jim and Meg. There was no way I could grab a towel and wrap it around me in time. Everything wrong with my body seemed more so with Jim there to see me in my bathing suit. My thighs were too heavy; my waist was too thick; and my breasts, which had grown too big, too suddenly, seemed to call too much attention to themselves. I finished the ice cream quickly and was the first one back into the water. Jim was next after me. We did handstands in the shallow end of the pool. I wasn't as good as my mom, but I could stay up the longest. I knew that Jim was watching me, and I kept my legs straight, my toes pointed.

Meg had what I thought of as a perfect body, tall and slim, but she didn't seem aware of it, just as she didn't seem to realize how pretty she was. Everyone in her family was really good-looking, but no one seemed aware of it. And no one cared much about what was in style.

My friends at home and I made it a point not to care about style—in our school there was a whole group of girls who cared about nothing else—but our moms all did. Meg's mom, Julie, wore old shorts and a baggy T-shirt. She never wore makeup, and her hair looked as if she had attempted to put it up in something like a twist but had been called away in the midst of her efforts. She wore no jewelry except a plain gold wedding band, and she smelled of whatever she was doing at the moment—cooking, or gardening, or putting sunscreen on a kid's back.

I tried to imagine Julie in the midst of a group of my mom's friends. I thought of them in their linen suits, diamond rings, and gold earrings, their faces made up, their hair professionally blown dry, their nails done, and always a little cloud of perfume around them as they moved.

Julie had been a professional dancer with a well-known dance company before she'd married, and you could tell from the way she moved, the way her feet touched the ground, the angle of her wrists, her chin.

"Mom wanted to be in a ballet company," Meg told me, "but she was too tall."

"Does she still dance?"

"No. But she teaches t'ai chi, and that has a lot of dance in it."

I knew about t'ai chi. My mom had tried it briefly at her gym, but had gotten impatient with it after a few weeks.

I saw Meg's dad only a few times. He turned up at the pool one particularly hot afternoon. He didn't look anything like Jim, but he was handsome too, with dark, curly hair, and the pale skin of a man who doesn't go outdoors very much. He was wearing faded blue bathing trunks, like my grandfather's. He climbed up on the diving board, did a few deep jumps that made the board arch more than I had ever seen it before, walked back and did a professional-looking dive approach, then landed in a cannonball that sent water shooting out all over the sides of the pool. He spent the next hour jovially throwing kids up in the air and spouting water like a whale. It occurred to me that he might not be sure which kids were his, which the neighbors', but it didn't seem to matter. The little kids climbed all over him, treating him like a large, inflatable toy.

When he climbed out of the water at last, his bathing trunks pulled down in the back, exposing a few inches of his white rear end. He hoisted up his trunks, retied them in front, slicked back his hair, and scooped up Meg's mom, who had been reading by the side of the pool. He carried her over to the water, while she laughed and kicked, swung her back and forth a few times as if he was going to toss her in, then jumped in with her in his arms. When she came up, spluttering and laughing, her hair was all loose and she looked like a mermaid. He set her on the side of the pool, kissed her on the mouth, hauled himself out of the pool, then went back inside the house to work.

✳ ✳ ✳

I had been riding my bike over to Meg's house, but on one rainy day my grandfather gave me a ride over. I called him when it was time to go home, but it was my mom who answered the phone and said she would come pick me up. I watched for the car from the front door. I told Meg I didn't want to keep her waiting. The truth was I didn't want my mom coming up to the house to get me. I knew she would want to take a look at Meg's mom and check out the inside of the house. I knew how her eye would be drawn to the sofa with the worn armrests, to the aluminum folding table set up by the window for a jigsaw puzzle, to the cheaply framed print on the wall (a Norman Rockwell, an artist my mom treated as a joke).

"My dad hung that up because he thinks that kid looks just like Stover," Meg explained when she noticed me looking at it.

"It does," I said.

I ran out to the car as soon as my mom pulled up.

"Hello, dear," she said, and she made a little kiss-kiss noise in my direction. She leaned forward over the dashboard to get a good look at Meg's house.

"Now that's unfortunate," she said. She pointed up at the profile of an air conditioner sticking out from a third floor window in Meg's dad's study. "They should install central air."

"I don't think they need it anywhere else. The house is pretty cool."

"But that ruins the lines. It's not our taste, of course, but a house like that has some character. What's it like inside?"

"Big," I said.

My mom circled around in the driveway and pulled out onto the street. "You've been over here every day for a week, Irene; I think it's time your new friend came over to your grandfather's house. Invite her to lunch. Or we could take her out to lunch. Serena's, maybe? It might not be wonderful for dinner, but I'm sure they'll have something you girls would like for lunch."

I didn't say anything. I couldn't imagine Meg facing up to a barrage of my mom's questions over lunch in a restaurant. I couldn't even imagine her having a meal with us at my grandfather's house.

"Next Wednesday," said my mom. "Invite her for Wednesday. I'll be going into the city with your father on Monday and we might stay over till Tuesday, but Wednesday should be fine."

I leaned my head back against the headrest and shut my eyes. My mom drove quickly and unevenly, braking hard when she went around curves. I always got carsick when she drove.

We pulled into the driveway. My mom turned off the ignition, but she didn't get out of the car. "I'd like to get to know this new friend of yours a little, since you seem to be spending so much time with her," she said. "She goes to the public school, doesn't she?"

"Mom, everyone around here goes to the public school. There is only one school."

"There's nothing wrong with public schools," said my mom. "Some of them are very good, in fact. But one does hear so much about what's going on in some of those places and—"

"Don't worry, Mom, Meg's not into drugs or alcohol or sleeping with guys or—"

"I wasn't imagining anything like that," said my mom.

"It's just that I want to make sure you're careful about the friends you select."

"*Select?* Select friends? I had friends, Mom; I had great friends, Eve and Frankie. They were my best friends in the world. But I'm not there anymore. You seem to forget that. You messed everything up and so I'm not home anymore and I'm not with any of my friends, so you don't have any right telling me to be choosy about the friends that I have now."

"Irene!"

But I didn't listen to her. I got out of the car and slammed the door behind me and ran up behind the house toward the barn. There was the old wheelbarrow, propped up against the wall by the ladder to my loft. I pulled down its handles and shoved it over. It crashed to the floor, knocking over a metal watering can. I kicked the can.

"Fuck you!" I shouted. "Fuck you!" I'd never really used that word before. I kicked the can, hard this time, and missed and stubbed my toe on the edge of the wheelbarrow. It hurt so much I felt dizzy and had to lean against the wall. When my toe had stopped throbbing I dragged myself up the ladder to my loft and lay on the loveseat. My crying was loud and raw and didn't sound like my own voice. It was as if there was a stranger in the loft beside me, a miserable stranger, sobbing and gasping for breath.

chapter nineteen

The next morning I went to Meg's house soon after breakfast. Theo came running out to meet me.

"We're making a circus, Irene," he told me, "and Bloomer is going to do tricks."

"What sort of tricks?" I asked.

"He's going to jump this high," said Theo, holding his hand up above his head. "And Stover's going to duggle!"

"Duggle?"

Meg came out behind Theo. She juggled imaginary balls in the air, and we both smiled.

"What's this circus?" I asked.

"It's for Mom's birthday," she said. "We did it once as a surprise for her and now it's become a kind of tradition."

I wasn't sure if I was should stay or not, and Meg caught the hesitation on my face. "You'll join us, won't you? Please?" she asked, immediately. "It's really for the little kids, I know, but Stover and Lolly need our help to get it going, and it's kind of fun. Jim's doing the setup and I'm doing costumes. Lolly is going to be a bareback rider. Stover's going to be a clown. He's got stilts, and he can actually walk in them. Jim and I will both be in the show too. Jim's the master of ceremonies."

"What are you doing?"

"Gymnastics. And the dog act. Will you do something with me?"

"I'm no good at gymnastics," I said.

"Just some cartwheels.

"I can't do a cartwheel."

"Sure you can," said Meg. "I'll help you. Watch. You just set your hand down like this, then kick your feet up." She did two perfect cartwheels across the lawn.

"Really," I said. "I can't."

Meg stood there, a pleading look on her face.

I looked around to make sure that no one was watching. I especially didn't want Jim to see me. "OK," I said, "I'll try." I did the best imitation of a cartwheel that I could, but it was more like putting my two hands on the ground and hopping to the side with both feet.

"See, I told you!" I said.

Meg did not laugh. "Maybe if I help hold your feet," she suggested.

We tried that, but ended up collapsing in a heap. This time we both laughed.

"It's hopeless," I said.

"Will you help with the dog act, then?"

"Maybe," I said. "What would I have to do?"

"Just hold up the hoop for Boomer to jump through."

"I guess I could do that," I said.

Jim was setting up the circus area in the side yard. He'd brought over lawn chairs and was making a circle on the grass with a length of garden hose. He looked up when we came over. It was funny what happened when he looked at me—I felt as if I had been running for a long way and was all out of breath.

"Good day, Irene," he said.

"Irene's going to help me with the dog act," said Meg.

"That's great," said Jim. "Now the only trick will be to get Bloomer to cooperate."

"Bloomer is a very cooperative dog," said Meg.

"Right!" said Jim. But Bloomer, who seemed to know we were talking about him, sat beside Meg and held his head up as if he had every intention of being the most co-operative dog in the world.

Lolly had arrived with her pony, Peaches. She boarded him with friends who lived out past my grandfather's house. Peaches was an old pony who had obviously been allowed to eat all the grain he wanted, and he looked particularly fat compared to Lolly, who was so incredibly thin.

"This is a really small circle, Jim," she said, as she started riding around. "We're going to get all dizzy."

"Just don't let him poop in the ring," said Jim. But it was already too late. Peaches was lifting his tail, right while he was trotting, and leaving a trail of manure behind him.

Meg took my arm, laughing. "Let's get out of here, quick," she said. We went upstairs to her room with Stover and Theo and worked on costumes for the show. Meg used face paints to give Stover a clown's face—white, with big sad eyes and a droopy red mouth. He wore a pair of his father's shoes on the wrong feet.

"Watch," he said, and he took three crayons and juggled them in the air.

"You're not going to try that while you're on stilts, are you?" asked Meg.

"I might," said Stover, and he winked at me.

Meg had made a tutu for Bloomer, but he kept trying to chew it when she put it on him. "We'll have to dress him at the last minute," she said.

We had two hula hoops for Bloomer to jump through. I covered one with paper and drew a picture on it of a dancing dog, with "The Amazing Bloomer" written underneath. The idea was that Bloomer would jump through the first hoop—each time I'd be holding it a little higher—and then as a finale he'd jump through the decorated hoop, bursting through the paper.

"How are we going to get him to go through the hoops?" I asked.

"Dog treats," said Meg.

Theo was digging through the piles of costumes on Meg's bed.

"I want to be a nelaphant," he said.

"You're going to be a lion," said Meg, and she held up a costume to show him. "Mom made it for him last Halloween," she said to me. "Isn't it cute?"

"I don't want to be a lion. I want to be a nelaphant," insisted Theo.

"Elephants in the circus don't say anything," I said, "but lions get to roar. Can you roar, Theo?"

Theo looked at me as if he wasn't sure he wanted to be taken in quite so easily. I got down on all fours and did some fierce roaring. Stover got on all fours and started roaring too. Theo couldn't resist. He got on all fours and joined the roaring, and Meg was able to get him into the lion suit (yellow flannel pajamas, with tail) and tie the lion's mane around his face.

"Thank you," Meg whispered to me.

Meg's father's face appeared in the doorway.

"We're practicing for the circus, Daddy," she said.

"Oh, right," he said. "Guess I better go get that ice cream for the party."

I ate lunch at Meg's house, and it was only when I was putting my plate in the dishwasher that I remembered I hadn't called my mother to tell her I wasn't coming home for lunch. All of the circus preparations had made me forget about my mother, made me forget how I had felt the night before, made me forget about my whole life. It was as if I was a different person as soon as I got off my bike and entered Meg's house. Fortunately it was my grandfather who answered the phone when I called.

"A circus!" my grandfather said, when I told him what we were doing. "What an enterprising family."

Meg was gesturing to me in the background. "Tell your grandfather he's invited," she said. "Your parents too."

"Meg says you're all invited," I told my grandfather, but he could tell from the tone of my voice that I wasn't eager for him to accept. I could just picture my mother, wearing a pair of stylish white slacks, her hair done just so, sitting on one of the Foxes' folding chairs with the frayed webbing, but not daring to lean back. She'd have a bright, determined smile on her face, but she'd be looking everything over, the way she always did.

After lunch Jim came upstairs to get his costume. Meg had found him a black cape and a black top hat and some white gloves that had come with a magician's set. He had a black mustache stuck to his upper lip, and he looked less like a kid with a fake mustache than himself, grown up.

He noticed the hula hoop I had decorated. "The Amazing Bloomer," he said. "Who thought up that?"

"Irene," said Meg.

"That's great!" said Jim. "Did you draw the picture too?"

I nodded.

"Not bad," said Jim.

I smiled and looked down, quickly. Suddenly there was a scream outside. It sounded like Lolly. We raced downstairs. Peaches had pulled himself free from the stake where he'd been tied up, and was standing, quite happily, in Julie's perennial bed with a clump of uprooted dianthus in his mouth. Lolly had grabbed his halter and was pulling him away, but the damage was already done. He'd eaten a lot of the plants and trampled the rest.

"I ruined Mom's birthday!" Lolly cried.

"It's Peaches's fault," said Stover.

"You can't blame Peaches," said Jim. "And it's not your fault, either, Lolly; it's mine," he said. "I didn't hammer that stake into the ground right."

We all stood there, staring at remains of the garden. Theo started to cry.

"What a birthday present for Mom!" said Meg.

"Maybe we could cover it with a big sheet, so she won't notice," said Stover. Everyone looked at him. He shrugged. "Just an idea," he said.

"We're going to have to replant it, somehow," said Jim. "But there's not much we can do now, before the show."

I didn't say anything, but I'd gotten an idea. I ran inside the house and called my grandfather and explained what had happened.

"What did she have there? Do you remember?"

"Dicentera, I think, and aquilegia," I said. "Dianthus in the front. I'm not sure what else."

"I'll see what I've got," said my grandfather.

※ ※ ※

The circus was a great success. At least Meg's mom thought so. She clapped at everything and laughed when things went wrong. We all did, especially when Bloomer refused to jump through either of the hoops and kept running around the side to grab his dog treats. As a finale he ripped off his costume and deposited it in Meg's mom's lap, his tail wagging, as if he was a retriever bringing back a prize. Meg's mom threw back her head and laughed so hard her hair clip came undone and her hair fell down around her shoulders.

My grandfather had arrived just in time for the show. He knew Jim and Stover, and I introduced him to everybody else. He'd brought a dozen plants with him. We placed them where the garden had been, and Meg's mom said they were even nicer than the ones that Peaches had eaten. Meg's dad wanted to pay my grandfather for the plants, but Grandpa insisted they were a birthday present.

"Besides, it's not every day the circus comes to town," he said.

My grandfather offered me a ride home after the ice cream and birthday cake. "I can throw your bike in the back of the truck," he said.

"I'll be home later," I said. "I need to stay and help clean up." I walked out to the truck with my grandfather. "Thank you for coming to our rescue," I said. "And thanks for coming to the show."

"Wouldn't have missed it."

"How'd you manage to keep Mom from coming?"

My grandfather looked down at his feet and reached to wipe some dirt from the toe of his boot. Then he looked straight at me.

"The truth is, Irene, I just said something to your mother about a delivery I needed to make. I didn't say much more than that."

I gave my grandfather a kiss good-bye and watched his truck back out of the driveway. Then I turned back toward the house. Meg had gone inside, but Jim was there, rolling up the hose that had been the circus ring. I stood for a moment and then, before I lost my courage, I took in my breath and walked over to him.

"Can I help?" I asked.

"Sure," said Jim. "Here, hold out your arms," he said. He placed the coiled hose over my bare arms and length by length added another loop.

"I like your grandfather," said Jim. "He's a really nice guy."

"Thanks," I said.

The hose was getting heavy, but I wished it was even longer. Jim circled my arms with the last loop and tucked in the metal end. He lifted the hose from me and slung it over his shoulder.

"You're really nice too, Irene," he said.

chapter twenty

My grandfather's pond was alive with creatures.
Turtles basked on fallen logs along the edges; salamanders swam lazily in the shallows; sunnies, pickerel, and
bass darted in and out of patches of sunlight. Their circling left round depressions in the sandy bottom of the
pond. The surface was covered with a myriad of insects:
skaters and boaters and damselflies. I hadn't known the
names of all these creatures—it was my grandfather who
taught me, just as it was my grandfather who first pointed
them all out to me. Before that the pond had just been a
territory of dark water, and all its inhabitants mysterious.

We spent Saturday morning getting the old canoe
ready to launch. The hull was all right, but my grandfather had to mend the wicker seats. I chased out a half
dozen daddy longlegs, then I washed the canoe inside

and out. I decided to name it the *Holden Caulfield*, after the character in *The Catcher in the Rye*, and I used a waterproof marker to inscribe the name on the bow. My plan was to get the canoe in the water and try it out, then later invite Meg over. And maybe, I thought, I could invite Jim too. I would ask them while we were all together so it would seem natural to include him in the invitation. There hadn't been any reason for them to come over before this, since it was their house that had all the things to do.

My grandfather couldn't find any paddles in the barn, so we went to the sporting goods shop in town and bought three.

"An extra for when one gets lost," he said.

They were beautiful wooden paddles, with curved handles that fit perfectly in your palm. The aluminum paddles were less expensive, but my grandfather said he'd rather paddle with his bare hands.

Just as we were heading to the register, my grandfather noticed a display of orange life jackets.

"I can swim, Grandpa," I said.

"I was thinking of your mother," said my grandfather.

"I'll never wear it," I said.

"Can't blame you," said my grandfather. He bought two flotation cushions instead. "You can sit on these," he said.

As soon as we got back home, my mom took the car and ran off to town on an errand of her own. She seemed excited and happy, and made a great deal over the secrecy of her mission. When she came back she produced a bottle of champagne.

My dad took a look at the label and his face turned sullen.

"Andie—," he began.

My mom kissed him on the lips. "It's a boat launching," she said. "It's an event."

"But you didn't need to buy champagne like this—"

"I won't let you spoil the fun," said my mom. "We have precious little to celebrate these days and we should enjoy every occasion we can."

My mom started rummaging through my grandfather's cupboards looking for glasses. She was surprised to discover two fine champagne flutes. "These are lovely," she said.

"They were a gift," said my grandfather, and I knew instantly, from the way he said it, who they were from.

"Well aren't you a man of surprises!" said my mom.

My dad took one end of the canoe, my grandfather, the other. I carried the paddles and the cushions and a folding chair. My mom led the way to the pond, the champagne bottle in one hand and a wicker basket with the glasses and napkins in the other.

The boat was lowered on the shore beside the pond, the cushions and paddles arranged inside, and then my grandfather pushed the boat out so only the stern was touching land.

"All right, Irene," my grandfather said. "Hop in."

I climbed into the boat and started toward the bow, holding on to both sides to keep my balance. I turned and sat down on the middle seat.

"Toast time!" sang out my mom. My dad opened the champagne and poured all around. I got a small glass full—a liqueur glass, etched with little flowers. My mom handed my grandfather a champagne flute, but he passed it to my dad and took a wine glass for himself.

"Toast!" cried my mom. "The *Holden Caulfield*!" I leaned far forward in the canoe so that everyone could clink glasses with me. The champagne was so tingly it was like drinking air.

"If this were a proper christening," said my mom, "we'd smash the bottle on the side of the boat, but I thought broken glass wouldn't be particularly desirable on the shore of the pond."

"Thank you, Andrea," said my grandfather.

"When I was a girl I went to a proper ship's christening," said my mom. "It was my uncle's boat—in Montauk. I was given the champagne bottle and shown what to do. I whacked it on the side of the boat, but the bottle didn't break. I whacked it again, harder, and the bottle didn't break. I gathered all my strength and whacked it a third time—but that bottle wouldn't break. Finally my uncle took the bottle and smashed it himself. Everyone laughed and applauded. Of course the champagne we drank came from bottles that had been opened the proper way."

"You've told us that story a hundred times," I said.

"That might be so," said my mom, "but this was certainly the perfect moment to tell it again."

I climbed all the way to the bow seat of the boat and my grandfather climbed in after me.

"Aren't you coming?" he asked my mom.

"Oh, no," said my mom. "I plan to wave from the shore. You go, Leland."

"I better be here to push us off."

"I can push you off," said my mom. So my dad climbed into the canoe, and my mom gave it a shove. We paddled around the small pond twice, then circled and paddled around in the opposite direction, waving extravagantly each time we passed my mom, seated on the shore. She waved the white dishcloth she'd brought for the champagne bottle.

The sun was the kind of glorious that makes you feel it reaches right in beyond your skin to your insides, and the day seemed as if it would go on forever.

Surely we were happy, I told myself. Surely this was the way it was supposed to be. Surely it didn't matter that the pond was small and muddy, that the champagne had been too expensive, that my dad had no job to go to when the weekend was over, and that my mom was working so hard to keep smiling and waving the white cloth.

chapter twenty-one

Meg came over on Monday, while my parents were in the city. Jim hadn't been home when I'd stopped by the day before to invite her. Although I'd said, as casually as I could, that Jim could come too, I wasn't surprised when she turned up alone.

With any of my friends from home, I would have been embarrassed to show them my grandfather's small, plain house, my own little room, but it was different with Meg. Eve or Frankie would have felt sorry for me, but Meg didn't see things the way they did, or the way I would. What she noticed about my room was the maple outside the window, a tree so old and huge it would take three of us, arms outstretched, to span it.

On my dresser she noticed a photograph in an oval frame.

"My grandmother," I said.

"She was beautiful, wasn't she," said Meg.

"I don't know," I said. "She died when I was little. I was named after her."

"I was named after Meg in *Little Women*. Everyone thinks my name is short for Megan, but it isn't."

"Did you like that book?"

"Not particularly," said Meg, laughing a little. "It went on too long, in places. But it had been my mom's favorite book when she was a girl."

"Why didn't she name you Jo?"

"I think she imagined she'd have a whole string of daughters, and she'd name the next one Jo, but then she had a boy next and gave up on the idea."

I thought about the next in line, who would be Beth. It would be dreadful to be named for her, first of all unreasonably good, then dead. The next girl in Meg's family was Lolly. No one said anything about it, but it seemed there must be something wrong with her. I thought of the illustration in my edition of *Little Women* of Beth lying on a sofa, shortly before she died. She looked a lot healthier than Lolly.

"Meg," I asked, "is there something the matter with Lolly? I mean, some reason she's so thin?"

"Oh, I thought you knew," said Meg. "But I guess you wouldn't, since you're new here. She has a congenital heart defect. But when she has her surgery, when she's a little older, they'll repair it and she'll be fine."

"But it's OK for her to be running around now, in the meantime?"

"There are two schools of thought about that. My mom believes that Lolly should be able to do whatever she wants to do, and that exercise will make her stronger."

"And your dad?"

"My dad says my mom's the one with the faith," she said, smiling. "So he leaves decisions like that up to her."

We went out to the barn to get the paddles for the canoe. Joppy heard our voices and came trotting over to check out Meg and say hello.

Meg squatted to pat him.

"I like his different colored eyes," she said. "What kind of a dog is he?"

"Mostly border collie—his coloring's called blue merle. Ideally he'd like a flock of sheep to herd. He has to be satisfied with herding us."

When I showed Meg my loft, she looked around it carefully then made herself comfortable on the loveseat. "What a wonderful place!" she said. "Are you allowed to sleep out here?"

"I don't know. I've never thought about it."

"I wish we had a barn," she said. "They're so reassuring. This is an old one, isn't it?"

"A lot older than the house. A hundred years or more."

"Before anyone alive today was born," said Meg. "Think about that."

"And it will probably be here long after anyone of us is still alive."

We looked at each other and laughed. The day was too sunny, the summer too certain, to think about anything like that. We headed off to the pond.

We paddled out to the middle of the pond, slipped the paddles back into the canoe and sat on the bottom with our legs draped over the sides, our feet in the water. The water was warm in spots, cool in others where I imagined there were underground springs. When the canoe was moving no more than our breath, the ripples smoothed and the surface became a flat black mirror for the sky and the trees surrounding us. One white birch bent down into the pond to touch its own image.

"Jim wanted to come today and try out the canoe," said Meg, "but he had too many jobs lined up. Can he come over another time?"

"Sure," I said. I tried to sound like it wasn't a big deal, but I was so happy I wanted to shout.

I dipped my hand in the water and slowly set the canoe moving in a circle. Meg was leaning back against the side of the canoe, looking at the world upside down. Suddenly she sat straight up and looked at me.

"There's something I sort of want to ask you," she said.

"Yeah?"

Meg waited a minute. "Do you like Jim?" she asked.

"Sure," I said.

"I don't mean that kind of like," she said. "Everybody likes Jim. I mean really like."

"I guess so," I said, and then, because she was still looking right at me, I added, "Yeah. I guess I do. Is that all right?"

A smile spread across Meg's face. "Of course it's all right," she said. "It's just what I had been hoping for. I think he likes you too."

I ran my finger along the smooth wood of the paddle. "You won't tell him, though," I said.

"Of course not," said Meg.

"Have you ever had a boyfriend?" I asked.

"No. Have you?"

"No. I had a crush on my social studies teacher, Mr. McClure, most of the year, but of course nothing could come of that. It was pretty stupid, really. Have you ever gone out on a date?"

"I went to the school dance with this boy who likes me. His name is Harlan. He once gave me a book of poetry by Robert Frost. I like Robert Frost. We went to the dance together, but he doesn't know how to dance, and I don't like to dance in public so mostly we stood there. So he doesn't really count."

"Of course he counts," I said.

"Even if I went with him more because I felt sorry for him than because I really wanted to be with him?"

"He counts," I said.

"What about you, do you go on dates?"

"No, not really. I go to an all-girls school, so I don't know any boys. My friend Eve matched me up with her cousin, and she went with a friend of his, and we went to a movie, but that was only once."

"Don't you have mixers with an all-boys Catholic school?"

"Catholic? I don't go to a Catholic school."

Meg looked surprised. "I thought you did. All girls, private—"

"But it's not a Catholic school. And I'm not Catholic, Meg."

Meg looked me at me as if she didn't believe me. "You're not?"

"No. What made you think I was?"

"You have a St. Christopher medal on your bike."

"Oh, that. It came with the bike. My grandfather bought it for me secondhand."

Meg lifted her legs over the side of the boat and shook the water from her feet.

"Does it matter?" I asked. "Does it matter that I'm not Catholic."

"Of course it doesn't matter," said Meg. "I just had assumed you were. But it doesn't matter. My own father isn't Catholic."

"He isn't?"

"No. Just my mom."

"But she's really religious, isn't she?"

"She goes to church three times a week, if that's what you call religious. And she raised us all to be Catholic. But she's fine about my dad not being a Catholic. And if we grow up and don't want to be practicing Catholics, she'd be fine with that also. She's already given up on Jim."

My mom came home from the city earlier than I expected. She came running over and called to us from the shore.

"Irene," she called, making my name three syllables. "Surprise!"

I paddled us in toward land.

"Marvelous luck, Irene," she said. "I think I've found us a place for the fall." My mom's face was radiant.

Meg jumped out of the canoe first and pulled it up on the ground, holding it steady for me while I walked forward and climbed out. We pulled the boat up onshore.

"Is this your friend, Meg?" my mom asked.

"Yes," I said. "Meg, this is my mom. Mom, this is Meg."

My mom extended her hand. Her diamond was glittery in the sunlight. "Call me Andie," she said.

Meg wiped her hand off on her shorts and held it out. She was taller than my mom, even with her shoulders slumped. They looked so odd holding hands, my mom still in her city heels, her hair, even after a day in the city and a long train ride, still falling in a smooth line to the bottom of her chin bone, her lipstick expertly applied—and Meg, who looked disheveled, a piece of a crumpled leaf adhering to her shoulder. She answered my mom's barrage of questions with such a soft voice my mom had to lean in close to hear her. I thought she might look over at me to rescue her from my mom's probing, from my mom's critical eyes, but she kept her eyes on my mom, smiling in her apologetic way.

It was a relief when my mom went back to the house.

"I'm sorry," I said. "My mom's just that way, so—"

"She's nice," said Meg. "She's really friendly."

"Overpowering, you mean."

"No, friendly. And she's so—elegant, like someone on TV."

I watched my mom walking back toward the house. It wasn't just the clothes she wore that made people say that about her; it was how she carried herself. She wasn't beautiful like Meg's mom, but you could imagine her interviewing people for the evening news, alert, crisp, absolutely sure of herself.

We turned the canoe upside down and started back to the barn on the path that cut through the meadow, each of us with the strap of the life preserver cushion over one shoulder and the paddle resting on the other.

"What did your mom mean about a place for the fall?" asked Meg.

I stopped walking. I'd been wondering if Meg had picked up on what my mom said.

"She's been apartment hunting in the city."

"Oh," said Meg, clearly disappointed, "I was hoping she meant she found a house around here. Not that you shouldn't stay here at your grandfather's, but I know sometimes people like their own place. But you have an apartment in New York already."

I looked at Meg. It seemed then that there was no way I could hold it all in any longer. There was no way I could go on pretending about what was really going on. I was tired of it, exhausted with it.

I sat down in the long grass, right where I was, and laid the paddle beside me. Meg looked at me, curiously, then sat down on the grass beside me.

"Here's the story," I said. "My dad lost his job back in the winter when his company merged with another. He's been looking for a new job, but hasn't found one yet. My parents had financial problems so we couldn't keep our penthouse anymore. So we came out here to stay at my grandfather's until we find someplace cheaper to live."

"Oh," said Meg. "I'm sorry."

I lay back in the grass and looked up at the sky.

"Our stuff is all in storage—and a lot of stuff got sold, and I won't be able to go back to my old school unless I get some sort of scholarship and I wouldn't want to do that."

"I'm really sorry," said Meg.

But I couldn't stop there. Once I began it just came pouring out.

"My parents have been fighting all the time and my dad is unhappy. My mom's unhappy too, I guess. And I don't know what's going to happen with us. I don't know what's going to happen about anything."

I turned on my belly and I cried. I cried into the grass, and the ground, and the earth. The ground smelled sweet and good, and the earth felt firm under my hands.

I cried until the crying stopped on its own. I sat up. Meg had been watching me, her face sad. "You could have told me," she said. "You could have told me right from the start."

"No," I said. "I couldn't tell anyone."

I got up and picked up the canoe paddle and the cushion. Meg got up also. We started walking back to the barn. "I'm glad you told me now," she said.

In the barn we hung the cushions on a peg that my grandfather had nailed there, and propped the paddles against the wall.

"I'm glad I told you too," I said.

chapter twenty-two

After Meg left I went into the house to find my mom. She was in the bedroom, in her bra and half-slip, hanging up the suit she'd worn into the city. She always wore lacy, uncomfortable-looking bras and matching silk panties and slips. Her suit jacket was perfectly square on its hanger, and the felt tabs that kept the skirt clips from pinching the fabric were perfectly aligned. Her shoes were by the side of the bed. They'd left a little red wedge in the top of each of her feet.

"So, you found an apartment?" I asked.

"I think I did," said my mom.

"Well, aren't you going to tell me about it?"

My mom took off her slip and stepped into her linen slacks. She zipped up the side zipper.

"Let's wait till dinnertime," she said, "so I can tell Daddy about it at the same time."

"Not even a hint?" I asked.

My mom pulled on a fitted T-shirt and smoothed her hair back off her face.

"It's on Sutton Place," she said, smiling. "And it's just charming."

"And we can afford it?"

"That's not for you to worry about, Irene."

"But, Mom—"

"I have it all worked out. It's an amazing bit of good luck—but not a word more. You'll have to wait till I tell your father about it."

I sat down on the end of the bed. I picked up the wooden shoe trees that were resting there and drummed them on the footboard. My mom took them from my hands and inserted them into her shoes.

"Meg seems like a pleasant girl," she said, "but unusually quiet."

"You barely gave her a chance to say anything, Mom. You just kept interrogating her."

"Interrogating? What a thing to say. I was showing interest in her, Irene."

"Well, she's shy, and you asked her a thousand questions."

My mom waved me away. She was in a good mood. "She seemed like a perfectly nice girl, Irene. And I'm happy you've made a friend for while we're here."

"I think I've made a friend for longer than that," I said.

My mom wasn't really listening to me. She gave her hair a few strokes with her hairbrush, leaned in toward the mirror over the dresser and examined a nearly invisible blemish on the side of her mouth, and headed off toward the kitchen.

The apartment, I learned at dinner, belonged to an old friend of my mom's who lived on some estate on Long Island, and kept it so she and her husband could have a place to stay when they came into the city for parties or shows. They were going to be living in London for the year, and were happy to let us use it while they were away.

"It's a beautiful little apartment, and it's fully furnished." My mom ended her recital, looking at my dad. "You remember it, Leland, don't you?" she asked.

My dad didn't look happy. "Can't say I do. I'm not sure I've ever been there."

"I'm sure you have," said my mom.

"You mean we won't have our own things out of storage?" I asked.

"Not for the time being," said my mom. "But that won't matter. The furnishings are exquisite."

"But I like my own things. Why can't we get a regular apartment, and have our own things?" I looked up at my dad. He was looking at my mom. I looked over at my grandfather. He was looking down at his plate.

"This apartment is a godsend, Irene. It's on Sutton Place, an ideal location. Apartments in that neighborhood are like gold."

"So, we'll live in another neighborhood."

"It's impossible to find a place in a decent neighborhood in Manhattan—everything's exorbitant, Irene. Don't think I haven't been looking."

"What about Brooklyn or Queens?" I asked.

"Queens?" asked my mom.

"Lots of people live in Queens, Mom," I said. "The whole borough is filled with apartment buildings and people live in all of them."

"Irene, we couldn't possibly live in Queens," said my mom. And she got up from the table and carried her dishes into the kitchen.

I looked at my dad. "Daddy?"

But he just shook his head.

"Daddy!" I shouted.

But all he would say was, "Let's just see how things go."

chapter twenty-three

Meg said all the kids wanted to see the pond, and I told her to come on Thursday, because my parents would be going into the city then. I could imagine what my mom's reaction would be to Meg's entire family trooping over.

I knew I'd been right as soon as they arrived, a parade of noisy kids, a tangle of bicycles dumped at the end of the driveway. They had nets and pails and fishing rods. Theo was wearing the life jacket that his mom made him wear whenever he was outside near the pool. He was bouncing with excitement and his white-blond hair, which was long and straight, flopped up and down. He had his heart set on finding a frog.

"A big frog, Irene," he informed me. "A big bullfrog frog."

Stover found a flat rock on the side of the pond and laid out his tackle and fishing gear. He was careful and methodical, and impatient with Lolly, who wanted a turn with the rod before he had it properly set up.

"Jim will be over later," said Meg. "He had stuff to finish at the house." I was grateful to her for telling me this so I wouldn't need to ask where he was. I was happy that I had that to look forward to, but it made me constantly hoping he would really come, constantly imagining him riding up on his bike, waving hello, walking across to us at the pond, his face in a ready smile. Otherwise it would have been a perfect afternoon, sunny and lazy and endless, the way summer days can be. Meg and I launched the *Holden Caulfield* and we took Theo on tours around the pond. He got to see two frogs, and Meg was able to persuade him that they were much happier in the pond than in a pail. Then we let Stover and Lolly have a turn in the canoe.

Meg and I stretched out on the shore and Theo went off with his pail to collect stones. That was Meg's idea to keep him out of trouble. "Small, pretty ones," she'd told him. I tried not to think about Jim. When he came, I didn't want to look as if I had been waiting for him. I wanted to appear casual, as if nothing had changed.

What had changed? Nothing, except that I had told Meg what I had only recently admitted to myself. I didn't feel different, but the telling made things different.

Liking Jim had turned into a fact, into something that had a life of its own.

When I heard someone coming up behind us, in spite of my plan to attempt to appear casual I spun around to say hello. But it was my grandfather who was smiling at us, not Jim.

"So, how're you girls doing?" he asked.

"Fine," I said.

"How's the yacht holding up?"

"It's still floating," I said.

My grandfather looked out at the canoe. "Ah, I see our young bareback rider and our clown are the current crew," said my grandfather, "and here comes our ferocious lion." Theo came running up to us, his pail banging against his knees.

"Look," he cried. "Look how many I got!" He set down his pail and very solemnly selected a pebble to give to Meg and to me.

"Theo, you should give one to Irene's grandfather too," said Meg, "since you found them by his pond."

"OK," said Theo, cheerfully. He rummaged in the pail and after examining and discarding several pebbles found one to present to my grandfather.

"Thank you very much, Theo," said my grandfather. He held the pebble up to show us. "An especially nice one. A bit of quartz with a fleck of mica in it." He slipped the pebble in his breast pocket. "I'll treasure this," he said to Theo, and he patted his pocket. The funny thing is that I knew he would treasure that stone.

My grandfather went back to the greenhouse. Stover and Lolly brought the canoe in and went back to fishing—they caught one sunny and threw it back—and we took Theo around again. He got to see not only more frogs, but a painted turtle. The turtle had been so perfectly posed on a fallen log that Theo thought it was a toy, until it looked up in alarm and plopped in the water. Theo let out a great squeal and jumped up in the canoe.

"Sit, Theo!" screamed Meg, as we grabbed the sides of the canoe to keep it steady.

As surprised by Meg's shouting—she rarely shouted—as the shaking of the boat, Theo burst into tears and we had to bring the canoe onto shore.

"He's getting tired. I'm taking him home," Meg mouthed to me when Theo's head was turned.

To him she said, "It's ice cream sundae time."

Theo looked expectantly at me.

"Back at our house," said Meg.

"I don't want to go."

I was about to suggest that we had ice cream and could probably make sundaes here, but realized what Meg was up to just in time.

"Mommy's got sprinkles. Chocolate and confetti sprinkles."

"Jimmies," said Theo. "They're called jimmies."

Meg looked relieved. She was able to steer Theo toward the bicycles.

Jim turned up just before they left. It wasn't at all as I had pictured it would be. I was busy trying to get the buckle undone on Theo's life jacket and suddenly Jim was there.

"We're going home for sundaes," Theo announced to him. "Chocolate jimmies too."

"I'm going back with Theo," said Meg. "Stover and Lolly are coming in a while."

"I'll stick around with them, then, since I just got here. I'm beat. Dad had me cleaning out the gutters on the carriage house."

"Dad?"

"Well, it was Mom who decided they needed to be cleaned out. But she didn't want me up on the roof without Dad there at the bottom of the ladder. The gutters on the house need cleaning out too, but they'll hire someone for that. Roof's too steep and those slates are slippery as hell."

As soon as Meg and Theo had left—Theo in the seat on the back of Meg's bike—Stover and Lolly decided to leave too. I was afraid that Jim would go with them, but he seemed eager to try out the canoe.

"Bow or stern?" I asked.

"Stern," he said. "I'll paddle you around, if you like."

"That would be fun," I said. I set the cushion on the bottom of the canoe and sat down there, facing Jim, leaning back against the seat. It didn't surprise me that Jim was as good at paddling as at everything else. He could turn neatly, back around, do figure eights. It occurred to me he might be showing off for my benefit, but then I thought not. It was just that Jim liked to do things well.

"Where'd you learn to canoe?"

"Camp."

"I didn't know you went to camp."

"Couple of summers. The trade-off was this year we got the pool put in, so we didn't do camp. Besides, I needed to stay home and work to make some money. I'm saving up for a car."

"That's kind of far off."

"Not so far. I'm getting my learner's permit next year. And I'll need to pay for the insurance."

Jim sounded so serious, like a grown-up, but then he grinned and stood up in the canoe and paddled gondola-style. He did a fine imitation of a gondolier, singing in fake or real Italian, I wasn't sure.

I lay my head back on the side of the canoe and shut my eyes for a second and imagined Jim. And then, when I opened my eyes he was still there.

After a while he sat down in the bottom of the canoe, and we just floated softly across the pond. Jim stirred the water with a paddle now and then to keep us out in the middle when we ended up too close to the side of the pond where the clump of birches hung low over the water, casting that part of the pond in shade.

"This is a great pond," said Jim. "Nice to skate on in the winter too. That is, if we have a winter when the ice isn't ruined by snow. You can try it out this winter, if you're still here. Will you be?"

"I don't know," I said. "Things are sort of still up in the air."

"It's a great pond, and a great place too. Hope Droisdale never gets his hands on it."

"Droisdale? Who's Droisdale?"

"This big developer around here. Buys up everything he can. I know he's had his eye on this place."

"How do you know?"

"When I was working here in the spring he came out one day to talk to your grandfather. Had those big blue plans unrolled out on the hood of his SUV."

"My grandfather isn't going to let his land turn into a housing development," I said. "He loves this place." I spoke with absolute confidence, but I was having trouble shaking from my mind the image of a developer unrolling plans for my grandfather. I was relieved when Jim turned my attention to the water beside the canoe.

"Salamanders," he said, pointing.

I looked over the side. The surface was black and opaque, a mirror for the sky, but by tilting my head and seeing it at a slightly different angle it turned into clear glass, and I could see right through. I saw a salamander where Jim pointed, then another, then several more. They were floating contentedly, a few inches below the surface of the water. Their tiny webbed paws looked like little miniature hands.

Theo's pail and little fish net had been left in the canoe. Jim filled the pail with water from the pond, and I took the net and managed, after several tries, to scoop up a salamander. When I went to dump it in the pail, though, it got caught in the netting, which was too wide, and in its struggle, tangled itself even more. I felt afraid it was hurting itself, afraid it was getting squished in the netting.

"Please," I said, "help!" I handed it over to Jim, and he carefully started to work the tiny creature free, but I couldn't stand to watch.

"Here, he's fine," he said, holding his hand out to show me.

"Just let him go," I said.

"Didn't you want to watch him in the pail?"

"No, please, just let him go."

"OK," said Jim. He released the salamander. "He's really all right, Irene," he said. "See?"

I looked over the side of the canoe. I had to lean way over to see below the surface. I spotted a big turtle swimming around the bow.

"Look!" I cried, and I pointed. I turned too quickly, and the canoe pitched, just as Jim was turning. The canoe rocked and I leaned in an attempt to steady it, and in one second I was feeling the boat slip out from beneath me, and in the next second I was plunging into the water, then spluttering up for air. Jim was right beside me.

✳ ✳ ✳

We come up, side by side, grabbing for the upside-down canoe. Hands, arms, shoulders, his, mine. I hold on to the side of the boat. Gulp air. All air. I can't get enough of it, and then, after a while, I start breathing again.

"You OK?" Jim asks.

"Yes. You?"

"Yup."

The water is warm on the surface, cold deeper below. I pull my feet up closer to my body.

"I'm really sorry," I say.

"Canoes. They do that."

We are close beside each other. Jim's hand is right next to mine on the side of the boat. So close that when he moves his a little, the outside edge rubs along the outside edge of mine. He slowly turns his hand outward so only thumb and forefinger are holding on to the boat. I do the same with mine. Mirror image. Our little fingers touch. Our hands move together so they are palm to palm. My whole body is there in my hand. Our fingers curl down between each other's fingers, holding fast.

Our hands push out into the water, away from the side of the canoe, and this pulls our bodies in closer together. We are each holding on to the boat with only one hand now. We are face close to face. Mouth close to mouth. Lips against lips.

Nothing will ever be the same again.

chapter twenty-four

Everything was different. The late afternoon light in my bedroom was pink and glowy. I lay on my bed and touched my lips with my fingers, carefully, slowly. It was as if I had never touched them before. I closed my eyes and brought myself back into those moments and went over them again and again, second by second.

My grandfather knocked on the door.

"Dinner in twenty minutes. If you'd like to help out, that wouldn't be objectionable."

I pulled myself up and joined my grandfather in the kitchen.

"I don't know which train your folks are taking. So we might as well go ahead and eat without them." My grandfather opened the oven so I could have a look.

"Eggplant parmigiana," he said, with a smile. "You can make the salad."

I took the colander out to the garden and gathered lettuce. My grandfather had planted a wide border of lettuce along a flower bed. There were all different varieties— some leaves were green, some reddish, some crinkly on the edges, some smooth. I pulled off the lower, outside leaves of a dozen different plants, careful to hold the plant so I didn't uproot it. I brought them into the kitchen and started rinsing them in the sink. The cold water on the leaves brought me back to the pond, and I let the water run over my hands so long my grandfather came over and turned off the faucet.

"Are you all right?" he asked.

"Fine," I said.

My grandfather gave me a smile that was a question.

But I couldn't tell him. I couldn't tell anyone just now, not even him, not even Meg. Though at dinner, the way my grandfather smiled at me, I wondered if it was possible that he knew, or guessed.

My parents had eaten in the city, but they eagerly took up my grandfather's offer for some ice cream for dessert. They seemed excited about something. I wondered if my dad had found a job.

"Let's wait till we're all sitting," I heard my mom whisper to my dad. I looked at my dad. He looked pleased about something, but still his face wasn't the face of a man whose worries were all over.

"We have a surprise for you, Irene," my mom announced when we were all at the table. "Daddy had some frequent flier miles, and we decided you could go out to Wyoming to visit your sister. We called Jenna and she was thrilled, so it's all worked out. When we were in the city today I saw our travel agent and she made all the arrangements. It's for a week. You'll be leaving this Sunday."

My mom looked over at my dad, as if they had rehearsed this part of it. "We know things have been kind of tough for you recently," said my dad. "We wanted you to have something to make your summer special." He produced an envelope from his pocket and laid it on the table in front of me. It was airline tickets.

Wyoming!

Of course I was happy, just as my parents expected me to be. Of course I couldn't wait to see Jenna. Of course this was the most wonderful, unexpected surprise imaginable.

But everything was different now. I didn't want to be going away. I didn't want be going one mile away from Jim and the Foxes and my life, what it had become. Two thousand miles were unbearable to imagine.

"Well?" asked my mom.

Everyone was looking at me. But I couldn't say a single thing.

"I think Irene's overwhelmed," said my grandfather.

My mom bounced up and came over to hug me.

"I knew she'd be thrilled," she said, looking back at my dad.

She was so happy, and my dad looked so happy too that I pushed out of my mind the angry feeling that I found coming up inside me, the feeling that my mom should have consulted me first, instead of planning my life for me. And I thought how my parents had really tried to give me something that they thought I wanted, and it wasn't their fault that because of something that had happened—something that they could never know about—I didn't really want it anymore.

"Thank you," I said. "This is wonderful. This is really great."

chapter twenty-five

Everyone at Meg's house was excited to hear about my trip. I felt a little guilty, as if I was going off and leaving them all behind, especially when Stover gave a great sigh and said, "How come we never get to go anywhere?"

"We went camping in the Adirondacks," said Meg.

"It wasn't that exciting," said Stover.

"What about the bears that got into our cooler?" asked Meg.

"It was night, so we never got to see them," said Stover. "You're going to see grizzly bears, aren't you, Irene?"

I shrugged. "Maybe," I said. "If I do, I'll take a picture for you."

"Will you take a picture for me too?" asked Theo.

"Of course I will," I said. "And I'll send you a postcard too."

"Just for me?" he asked.

"I'll send one to each of you," I said, and I caught Jim's eye. I couldn't write anything personal on a postcard, but I wanted to be able to send one to him alone.

When it was time for me to go home Jim said he was going in that direction and we could ride part of the way together. From Meg's smile, I wondered if this had been her suggestion, if she had conspired with Jim a moment when I was out of the room. She hugged me good-bye and herded the rest of the family out in back for a swim.

Jim and I got our bikes and headed off together. He rode right alongside of me, keeping exactly with my pace, slowing with me on the uphills, and flying with me on the downhills, braking as I braked, as if we were two people on a tandem bike. The sound of his breathing and my breathing, the sound of his pedaling and my pedaling, the sound of his gears shifting and my gears shifting—all these sounds blended together.

We were too soon at the corner of my grandfather's property, the driveway not far ahead. I came to a stop and stood, straddling my bike. Jim stopped beside me. We were so close the ends of our handlebars were touching. Our forearms brushed against each other. We both looked out over the fields and the pond. The greenhouse, the barn, the house were like toy buildings in the distance. We pressed closer, so we were arm against arm. Jim looked quickly up the road in each direction, but there were no oncoming cars. He leaned toward me and kissed me. He kissed me twice.

When I opened my eyes he was smiling at me.

"Have fun in Wyoming," he said.

"OK," I said. "I will."

We stood for a while longer. A car came along the road and seemed to slow for a moment when the driver saw us, then it sped past.

"Guess I better be going," I said. I spun the bike pedal backward so it was set for my foot.

"See you soon," I said.

"See ya."

Jim stayed there, at our spot, and waited while I biked down the road and up the driveway. I didn't look back while I was biking, but I was certain he was watching me. I leaned my bike against the side of the barn. I heard my mother's voice in the house and stepped quickly out of sight, into the shadow just inside the barn door. I watched Jim get on his bike and turn around and ride away, beyond the curve in the road.

chapter twenty-six

From all the postcards Jenna had sent me of Yellowstone, I had an idea of the scenery, but I had no idea how big everything was. The post-cards—even the views of meadows with distant moun-tains or giant waterfalls—were, after all, only the size of a postcard, something I could hold in one hand. But in real life these vistas stretched out so far it seemed as if you could never reach the end of them. My grandfather's farm and the pond, in comparison, seemed small as a children's play yard, and I was tinier than I had ever felt myself to be. Jim seemed like a world away. I carried him in me, a secret in my mind, but I had to work to hold on to him, like protecting an ice cube in my fist on a summer day.

Yellowstone was called a park, and so I'd imagined New York's Central Park—rugged, bigger—but still something contained. But Yellowstone was as big as an entire country; it just went on and on. I could lay the postcards side by side, but the sights of Yellowstone were hours and hours apart from each other. Jenna, in the battered Volvo wagon, a hand-me-down from her father, was determined to show me as much as possible. She'd taken some days off from her research project—studying bighorn sheep out in the wilds of Montana.

"Is that OK?" I asked.

"It's good. It's great," she said. "I needed some time back in civilization."

This made me laugh. We were staying in a tiny log cabin deep in the woods, in a small clearing with a lodge and cabins all close around it. It seemed like an outpost in the wilderness. There was no running water or a toilet or electricity. There were two beds, a table and one chair, and a wood stove in the corner. When we got into our beds and turned off the flashlights it was darker than any place I had ever been. The cabin smelled like Christmas. Summer felt far away.

"Are you warm enough?" Jenna asked.

"I'll be OK."

In fact, I was cold, but I knew if I said anything Jenna would get up and make a fire in the stove, and I knew how tired she was from driving all day, from making arrangements, from showing me around. She'd taken me to see hot springs and geysers, bears and buffalo (which, Jenna explained, should be called bison). Making up to me for all the things I had never seen. Making up to me for all the years when she lived so far away and wasn't much of a sister to me at all. Making up to me for what had been going on in my life, everything that had been taken away.

During the day, with all the adventure before us, I'd forgotten about my life, forgotten about who I was, really. At night now, something like homesickness came over me. But what was I homesick for? Our penthouse in the city, my old life? Or my grandfather's house, what my life had become? Maybe I was no one. Maybe I had no home at all.

"So," Jenna whispered. "What's this new apartment like?"

"I haven't seen it yet. I think Mom said we'd go into the city and have a look at it when I got back."

"What's happening with your school?"

"I don't know," I said.

"I guess it will depend on your grandfather."

"What do you mean?" I asked.

"Whether he comes up with the scratch."

"Grandpa? I don't think he has that kind of money."

"No, but he has all those assets."

"Assets?"

"All that land. He could sell it off, make a fortune. I think that's what drives Mom crazy."

"But it's his business."

"He'd invest the money and he wouldn't need to work."

"But he likes to work. It's what he does. And where would he live?"

"I suppose he could still live right there, in the house, and the land could be developed around him."

I thought of my grandfather's house surrounded by large, new houses, the fields, the greenhouse, the barn all gone. I sat up in bed.

"Jenna," I cried out, "do you really think that's what he should do?"

"God, no," said Jenna. "I don't think your grandfather should touch that place. I was just explaining what I think Mom's so frustrated about. She thinks your grandfather is—well, never mind."

"What?" I asked. I found the flashlight on the bed stand between us and flipped it on. "What? Tell me."

"Mom thinks your grandfather is selfish, that's all."

"What does she want?" I asked.

Jenna laughed a little. "I guess ideally she'd want your grandfather to turn everything over to Lee, and for him to have the property developed. That would bail them out, for the moment at least. Since of course you know Mom. No matter how much cash she has available, she'll find a way to run through it. She's always been an expert at confusing luxuries for necessities."

I thought about some of my mother's luxuries. Maybe what seemed like luxuries were necessary for her. Maybe she needed those things to keep her going, keep her who she was.

I looked at Jenna. When we were up, walking around, she looked a lot like Mom—she was petite like her and walked the same way—but her face now by the small light in the room was a very different face, not pretty like Mom's, with big, green eyes and fine nose, but like her father's, with his heavier features.

"You don't think my grandfather would ever give up a piece of that place, do you? Why would he?"

Jenna pushed her hair back over her ears and cupped her face in her hands. "He might," she said. "If Mom persuaded him it was for you. If it meant having the money so that you could continue in your private school, so you could have all the things you've had to give up. She'll work on him. She'll work on Leland to work on him."

I thought about my grandfather back there at the farm with my mom and my dad talking to him when I was far away. Maybe that was why my mom sent me to Yellowstone, so she could work on my grandfather without me around.

I lay back in the bed. I felt sick.

"I hate her," I whispered.

"Don't say that. You don't really mean that."

I had said it without thinking about it. It surprised me now. Did I mean it? I didn't know.

"How do you feel about her?" I asked after a moment. "Don't you hate her too?"

"No. She's just the way she is. You just have to come to accept that. "

"Did you always?"

"God, no! When I was your age—"

"When you were my age, what?"

"Well . . . it's a long story. There was a lot going on then. Mom met Leland. She wanted to snare him as a husband. Mom shipped me off to live with my father."

"I thought you had gone to live with him because it was his turn. Because that's what the custody agreement was."

"Not exactly. She could have kept me if she wanted to, but it was much more convenient if she didn't have me to deal with. Newlyweds don't exactly need a kid from a previous marriage underfoot."

"But I know Dad always loved you, Jenna. He's always wanted you."

"Your dad is a darling, Irene. No, it wasn't Leland; it was Mom. She didn't want to be encumbered. She's never been one to want to saddle herself with children, to saddle herself with anything. You know that."

"She saddled herself with me," I said, simply.

"You were different. You were the product of her new marriage. I was the leftover from the one she outgrew. And the truth is, Irene, when you were little she left the real work of raising you to hired nannies."

I thought about this for a moment. I thought about when I was a kid, how I never understood why my big sister never really lived with us, why she came home only for holidays and visits. I remembered how I kept a set of markers and a big drawing pad in her room and how I used to go there when she was away and lie on the floor and draw and pretend that she was there with me, just reading on her bed. Sometimes—oh, I hated to remember this! I tried to push the memory away, but it came ferociously back—sometimes I even talked to her, as if she were there. And once Mom came into the room and caught me and asked me whom I was speaking to and I said, "It's a secret," because it was.

I reached across the space between the beds and took Jenna's hand. "I missed you all those years, Jenna," I said. "I wished you had lived with us all the time."

"I missed you too," she said.

chapter twenty-seven

I bought postcards wherever we went. I sent postcards to Jim and Meg and Stover and Lolly and Theo. I
sent postcards to my parents and my grandfather. I sent
postcards to Eve and Frankie. And I sent postcards to
every single girl I knew at school. They were the kind of
postcards other girls sent out in the summer to their friends
at school—postcards from people who had gone places,
who were really on vacation. I couldn't have sent them
postcards from my grandfather's house in the country.

I kept a list of all the animals I saw. I had two bears,
one coyote, two bison, a herd of elk, and dozens of whistling pigs (otherwise known as ground squirrels, but who
would want to call them that?). I kept a list of all the license plates from all the states. I had them from thirty-
eight states, including one from Alaska.

There weren't many cars from New York. At one parking lot we parked next to a station wagon with New York plates. As we were getting out of our car, the family was returning to theirs: a mother, father, brother, sister, all wearing glasses, caps with visors, and running shoes. The kids stood by the car licking ice cream cones while the parents were securing the car-top carrier. They must have driven all the way from New York, covering mile by mile all the land that I had witnessed, so quickly, from the window of the plane as I flew over it all. They might even have looked up at night and seen my plane, a tiny, blinking spot, making its way across the sky.

I thought about saying hello to the "glasses" family and telling them I was from New York too. But that seemed silly. There were a million people from New York—even if not that many of them were in Yellowstone. And if they asked me where I lived in New York, what would I say? Did I live back where I used to live or at my grandfather's house in the country or some apartment which I hadn't even seen yet?

Jenna's car had Montana plates, and I liked that. I liked the idea that people would think I was really from out here, that I really belonged to this vast place called the West. I liked the fact that my New York identity was a secret until I chose to reveal it.

The back of the New York car was packed with camping stuff: a cookstove, cooler, gear, duffel bags. The glasses family, the four of them all dressed alike, looked

as if they were totally self-sufficient, as if they had everything they needed for the longest trip, for forever.

"OK, Marty, Ezra, hop in. We're off," the father said,
and four car doors opened and slammed shut. The car
started up and backed out of its spot, with all four of them
neatly tucked inside.

My parents had never taken me on a cross-country trip,
never would. It was fun to be out here with Jenna, to be the
two of us on our own, but I also wished I were part of a family like the glasses family, a perfect family of four on a typical
American vacation, all four of them snug in the car together.

It was a day for waterfalls, for the scenic views of the Grand
Canyon of Yellowstone, which is a gorge with the Yellowstone
River deep at the bottom. Jenna had picked out a trail that
took you all the way down, as the map showed, into the canyon. It was 800 feet from top to bottom, like dropping off a
cloud onto the earth below. Signs warned people with weak
hearts not to attempt it because of the difficulty of the climb
back up. I put my hand to my chest where my heart beat,
young and healthy. I thought of Lolly. Surely this was one activity even Julie would prevent her from trying.

I had no trouble at the top of the trail, though I felt nervous where the trail was too close to the edge. But then we
came to the part that went straight down on the side of the
canyon. There was a metal staircase against the rock wall,
switchbacks of open-work grating, like a fire escape, that
let you see right through. I suppose it was so that rain could
drain through, or maybe it was just the way the grillwork

was constructed. At first it seemed sturdy enough. I went down one flight, then another, to a landing. But then the stairs seemed to hang out more over the drop-off, and rather than be attached to the wall of rock they seemed to depend on spindly supports. I could see down through the grating.

Sweat soon covered my forehead and collected in a mustache above my lip. I wiped my face and neck with the bottom of my shirt. I was feeling a little dizzy and feverish. The view below me started swimming. I knew the metal staircase was firm beneath my feet, but once I imagined it moving, I could almost feel it sway. I felt as if I were walking on air itself.

I gripped the handrails on either side of me. Jenna was ahead of me, a dozen stairs below. When she realized I wasn't right behind her, she turned to look back at me. "Are you OK?" she asked.

I made my way cautiously to the end of the run of stairs. A bench had been built into the switchback. I sat down.

"I'm kind of tired," I said. "Would you mind going down the rest of the way without me? I'll wait here for you."

"We don't have to go all the way down," said Jenna. "If you don't want to, we can head back up now."

"But we've come so far," I said. "Why don't you go, and let me stay here?" I thrust my camera toward Jenna. "And take a picture for me when you get to the bottom."

"Are you sure?" Jenna asked.

"I'm sure," I said.

"Will you be all right here?"

"Of course."

"OK," she said. "It's probably only about ten minutes down and back. You'll stay put?"

"Yes," I said.

She handed me the binoculars. "Here, take these. You can look around while you're waiting."

Once she was gone I leaned my head back against the rock wall and shut my eyes for a few minutes. Hikers were trotting down the stairs in front of me, others laboring up. I tucked my feet in close.

I opened my eyes when someone plopped down on the bench beside me. It was a fat man with a baseball cap. He was panting and sweating and smelly. I moved over on the bench to make room between us. He took off his cap and fanned himself with it. The top of his head was bald, and the fringe of hair that circled it was drenched in sweat. He was wearing a tank top, but he must have been wearing a short-sleeved shirt the day before because his arms were sunburned up to the sleeve line.

"What a climb!" he said. "Nothing for you young ones, I know, but let me tell you, this one nearly did me in."

He didn't seem to expect a response, and I didn't feel like talking. Would I tell him that I hadn't been down at all? That in fact I hadn't really earned a place on the bench?

"Well, time to hit the trail," he said after a while, and he pushed himself up with a gasp.

I was relieved to have him gone at first. But later a breeze started up, and I felt as if the staircase was swaying again, and I wished that large, substantial body was still there next to me.

It seemed as if Jenna had been gone a long time. I had no watch with me, but surely it was longer than ten minutes. Twenty minutes, maybe. I lifted the binoculars and had a look. It was a terrible mistake. The distant view was instantly in front so I felt as if I was falling right into it, and when I shifted back to the world around me, everything spun. My stomach churned.

"Jenna," I whispered. "Jenna, come back."

Could she have been gone for hours? What if she never came back?

A group of people was coming up the staircase—a family with a half dozen children, dressed in old-fashioned cotton clothes, Amish probably. Had they passed me on the way down while my eyes were shut, or had they been a long time at the bottom? I thought about asking them if they'd seen Jenna down there, but how would I describe her? A young woman in jeans shorts with a blue bandanna holding her hair off her face? They were gone, bounding up the staircase. The littlest girl, next to last in line, turned to look at me. She said something to her older sister, who looked back, and pulled her along. The staircase seemed to shake as they went past.

The rock wall behind me is the only thing that's secure. The staircase and the landing where I sit seem as untethered as an orbiting space station. I have to get off. I have to get back onto solid ground.

I rise shakily to my feet and take a step toward the stairs. I grab onto the handrail and press my body as close as I can to the side of the canyon wall.

"Don't look down. Don't look down," I tell myself. I begin to climb. I keep my eye on my hand on the handrail. I do not let myself turn my head out toward the view or down toward my feet. I climb as quickly as I can, but when I start to stumble I make myself slow down. My heart is pounding so furiously it's hard to breathe. The stairs are endless in front of me. I feel as if I'm underwater, drowning, groping my way up to the surface.

But it isn't as far as I had imagined, because suddenly I am at the top. There is solid ground beneath my feet. There is a bench, a wooden bench, set back from the edge. I sink down onto it. My face is wet with either tears or sweat or both.

Finally Jenna turned up.

"What happened?" she asked. "You were supposed to be waiting back there."

"I couldn't stay there any longer," I said, but she wasn't listening. Her face was red and she was panting. She looked upset. "Why'd you leave?"

"I thought you were never coming."

"Of course I was coming. I just took two pictures and came right back. You said you'd stay where you were."

"You shouldn't have just left me—"

"Irene, you told me to!"

"Well, I didn't know you'd be gone that long," I said.

I was angry at Jenna, even though logically I knew I had no reason to be. I was angry at her for leaving me even if I had insisted that she do just that. She should have known what would happen. Shouldn't she? Wasn't she supposed to protect me from things, even the things that I didn't know would turn out to be a problem? Wasn't anyone ever going to protect me?

Jenna sat down beside me. She took off her bandanna and shook her hair free. "When I didn't see you there, Irene," she said softly, "I panicked for a moment. I didn't know what had happened to you."

"I couldn't stand waiting there. I was all dizzy. I had to get back up on land."

Jenna looked at me. "I didn't know you were afraid of heights," she said. "Why didn't you tell me?"

"I didn't know. I mean, before this I never thought I was." I thought for a moment about our penthouse terrace. We were so high up there and I used to stand right by the wall looking out at the city so far below me, and it never bothered me at all. Something was different now, something about me had changed. "It's just this was so—"

"Oh, Irene!" cried Jenna, and she put her arms around me. "I'm so sorry! I never would have abandoned you there if I had known!"

chapter twenty-eight

It was my dad who picked me up at the airport. I spotted him before he saw me. He was a head taller than the family that was in the crowd in front of him. They were jumping and waving and calling out to some passenger who was ahead of me, and he looked like a grave schoolteacher at the back of a group of noisy schoolchildren. When he finally spotted me his face broke into a smile.

"Well, look who's here!" he said when I made my way over to him. He gave me a quick hug, pushed me a shoulder's distance away from him and looked me over, then hugged me again. "Hi, sweetheart," he said.

"Hi, Daddy."

"I like the hat," he said, as we walked over to the baggage claim.

"Jenna got it for me," I said. It was a cowboy hat, not the kind they make for the tourists, but the real kind. I put it on his head. It was too small, but it was a style that looked good on him.

"I would have bought you one, Daddy, but I didn't think Mom would approve. She'd think it's not—" I was about to say "corporate enough," but I stopped myself in time. "—not you," I said.

My dad shrugged. He looked so much like my grandfather. Then I realized it was also because he was wearing old jeans, a work shirt, and the heavy boots he wore when he was working on the stone wall. I was surprised my mom let him come into the city dressed like that.

He caught me looking at the boots and grinned. "I know what you're thinking, Irene," he said. "And the answer is I snuck out of the house without her seeing me."

I laughed.

"Did you get anything decent to eat on the flight?" he asked.

"It was OK," I said.

"I was thinking by the time we get back to the house it might be getting late. We'll be hitting rush hour traffic. Might make sense to catch something here—unless you're not hungry."

I had the feeling that my dad really wanted to stop by a restaurant before we drove back, so I said I was a little hungry.

I ordered a grilled cheese sandwich, because I knew that's something that even an airport restaurant can't goof up, and I ordered iced tea, because that's what Jenna always drank.

"Same for me," said my father, which surprised me, because he never drank iced tea.

"Wait till we get back to the house to tell about Jenna and your trip, because your mother wants to hear all about it."

"I can tell her too," I said.

"Not the same thing as hearing it fresh," said my dad.

"Why didn't she come to the airport, then?"

"She intended to," said my dad, "but it was clear she wasn't going to be ready on time. And I thought you'd like to have someone here to meet the plane when it landed."

"Thank you, Daddy," I said.

It was typical of my mom. She was always running late, always expecting people would wait for her. Usually they did.

"You did have fun, though, didn't you?" my dad asked. "At least you can tell me that."

"I had a great time," I said.

"And Jenna. How's she doing?"

"She's good," I said. "She brought me everywhere, Daddy. I took a zillion pictures. I can't wait for you to see them."

Our grilled cheese sandwiches were the thinnest I'd ever seen. My dad lifted back a corner of his and peered inside.

"I think there might be a sliver of cheese in here somewhere," he said. "Well, nothing so bad that a little mustard can't cure it."

The mustard came in a yellow plastic squeeze bottle, the kind Meg's family used. My dad peeled the top layer off the sandwich and squeezed a big yellow snake of mustard over the bottom layer. The plastic bottle made rude noises when he squeezed it, and we both laughed. The mustard my mother bought came in small jars with labels in script, and it was brown and grainy.

When my father put the sandwich back together, mustard oozed out the sides. Even though he used a knife to skim it off, he still ended up with mustard on his face when he took his first bite.

Our iced tea was served with straws in paper wrappers. I pushed the wrapper down around the end of mine and held it there while I blew into the straw. The accordion pleats unfolded so it looked like a live white worm. My father took a quick look around, then he did the same thing with his straw. I could just imagine what my mother would say if she saw us.

※ ※ ※

When we headed north out of the city, I thought about us driving to my grandfather's in that rented car at the start of the summer. It hadn't been that many weeks ago, but it seemed as if that day was as far away as it could be and have me still be able to remember it. My grandfather's house had been some remote place that we were escaping to. Now it felt as if I were going home.

I leaned my head against the window.

"Tired?" my dad asked me.

"Uh huh," I said. But it was the nice kind of tired. The kind of tired when you've done a lot and aren't in any hurry to get anywhere.

"By the way," said my father, "your friend Meg called yesterday and asked that you call her when you get back. One of the kids in her family is in the hospital."

I sat up. "Who is it?" I asked. "What happened?"

"I'm sorry; I don't know anything more about it," said my dad. "Your mother is the one who spoke to her, and I gather Meg was in a hurry and didn't say much."

"It's Lolly. Must be. She's Meg's little sister. She has a problem with her heart, but she wasn't supposed to have surgery till she was older. Something must have happened."

"Don't worry, sweetheart," said my dad. He reached out and stroked my head. "It's probably nothing too serious."

But I was afraid that it was. I thought of Lolly, when I last saw her, pale and horribly thin. I could picture her lying in a hospital bed, her dark eyes too big for her face, her dark hair spread around her head on the pillow.

The whole plane ride my mind had been alternating among three things. I had been thinking of Jenna, saying good-bye to her, knowing I wouldn't be seeing her again for a long time, missing her already. I had been thinking of my grandfather's property and hoping I got back before he made any deals with a developer. And I

152

had been thinking of Jim, and how it would be to see him again.

This news wiped everything from my mind. All I could think about now was Lolly, gasping for breath. I pictured her mom praying at the side of her hospital bed and her dad pacing back and forth in the intensive care unit. Meg and Jim huddled with Theo and Stover in the waiting room—for they wouldn't allow kids in the intensive care unit. Or would they? Maybe if your sister was dying they'd allow you in.

It seemed a fortunate thing for Meg that both she and her mom were practicing Catholics. My old friend Frankie's family was Catholic, and I knew that being Catholic offered you the activity of prayer, a useful occupation when there was nothing else to do, and it also offered you a degree of hope. Being Catholic meant there was not only a benevolent God you could appeal to, but also Christ and the Virgin Mary, and a whole collection of assorted saints. If you had to face trials in life, it seemed as if Catholics were better armed than the rest of us. If there was anything that I envied Meg, it was that.

When I got back to my grandfather's house I barely said hello to my grandfather and my mom before I ran to the phone and called Meg. All I got was their answering machine. I'd never heard the message before. Someone had picked up every time I'd called. It was Theo's voice, with some coaching in the background. "This is the Foxes. We're not here now. So call us back or leave a message when you hear the beep." He beeped, himself, several times and a voice—Jim's?—in the background said, "OK, Theo, enough." The message was a happy kid's voice, the voice of a kid who believes everything is all right. A voice from a time when that was so, a voice frozen in the past. A voice that lied.

"This is a message for Meg," I said. "Meg, it's me, Irene. I'm back. Call me!"

It was dinnertime, but I didn't feel like eating. I kept waiting for the phone to ring. My parents and grandfather wanted to hear all about my trip and about Jenna, so I told them about things, but I didn't feel much like talking. Yellowstone felt as far away as a distant planet. Was it possible that I had been there only the day before?

The next morning I waited until nine thirty for Meg to call; then I called her number again. It was the same message on the answering machine, Theo's voice bright and happy.

My parents went into the city for the day. My mom suggested I go with them since there was a chance they might go by the new apartment. I wanted to stay and wait for Meg to call me.

But she didn't call, not all morning. Maybe she hadn't gotten my message. Maybe she didn't know I was back. I called and left her another message. My grandfather asked me to help him in the greenhouse. There was a phone extension out there, and I stayed close to it because I was afraid I might not hear the ring over the noise of the fan.

I was weeding pots of asters, plucking out the frail beginnings of other plants, thin blades of crabgrass, whatever was daring enough to start a life on the side. I liked weeding. I liked the certainty of it. You could pull up a weed and it was really gone, and when you patted the soil flat from where you had plucked you couldn't even tell that anything had been there. The greenhouse was warm and moist and comforting, but my attention was still on the phone, which refused to ring.

I wiped the soil from my hands and called Meg's number once more. I hung up as soon as I heard the start of Theo's message. Maybe they had the volume turned way down so they weren't hearing any calls. Maybe there was something wrong with their phone and Meg had been waiting all this time for me to call.

My grandfather was watching me.

"Would you like me to give you a ride over to Meg's house?" he asked.

"Thanks, Grandpa," I said. "I think I'd like to bike over there, though. Do you think that's OK?"

"I think it's fine." His hands were covered with potting soil. He held them out to the side and leaned down and kissed me on the top of my head.

I biked as fast as I could, and it felt good to be doing something, to be moving. It had never seemed farther to Meg's house. It was as if someone had taken the landscape and stretched it out, made each familiar landmark farther from the next. I kept picturing Lolly, her pale face against a pillow which got whiter and whiter in my imagination. It felt as if I were racing to reach her in time. In time for what?

When I got to the front walk of the house I stopped short. There were no cars in the driveway and the house looked all closed up. The front door, heavy as a door on a medieval castle, was firmly shut and the windows were all shut too. The place was dark and quiet, and the toys and equipment that were usually scattered around the lawn and porch were all out of sight. There was such an air of silence and desolation I didn't even go up and ring the bell. It didn't seem like a house I had ever been in before. It didn't seem like a house that was inhabited by kids. I thought of that first day when I met the Foxes, the day when the house had opened up to me, when it had turned from a stone mansion into the home of friends.

But I wasn't ready to just leave. I propped my bike on the kickstand and walked around to the back of the house. The pool lay quiet and unused, the diving board absolutely still, the lounge chairs empty. A single ball had floated to the corner of the shallow end and gotten wedged by the wind under the concrete molding.

I stood there for a while, staring up at the house, window by window, to see if I could discern any sign of life. Then I heard a car in the driveway. I peaked around the corner. It wasn't either Meg's family's van or her dad's car. Immediately I felt frightened, as if I had been trespassing. How could I explain my presence? I thought I might just sneak off, duck behind the rhododendrons and make a run for the street across the lawn, but my bike was there, glaringly out in front of the house. It was a long walk back to my grandfather's if I decided to just abandon it there.

The car pulled up right in front of the house and stopped. The doors opened. Jim got out of the car. Meg got out of the car. A woman who looked so much like Meg's mom I thought at first it was her, got out of the car. She lifted Theo out of the car. Then Lolly got out of the car. She looked fine—she looked just the way she always looked. I flew across the lawn to meet them.

chapter twenty-nine

We imagine things. We imagine them so well, in such detail, that we almost bring them into being by our imagination. Then, when reality hits, and it's entirely contradictory, we feel at first that it must be a mistake.

The Lolly I had seen in my mind was my own creation. Her pale face against the pillow, her dark hair spread out around her—making her face smaller and whiter—wasn't her at all, didn't touch her in any way.

It was not Lolly who had been in danger at all. She hadn't even been sick. The one who was in danger was Stover. It was Stover—strong and sturdy in my imagination—who had been in the intensive care unit. It was Stover at the center of the hospital scene, and it was Lolly who was standing beside the bed, not lying in it. It was

Stover who was as close to death as a person can be who is still alive.

"What happened?" I asked, as soon as Meg told me the news.

"He was on his skateboard, on his way home from a friend's house on the other side of town. Someone ran into him . . ." Meg's voice broke. She pressed her fist against her mouth. ". . . and they didn't even stop! He was unconscious till this morning. We didn't know if he would make it. But he did."

"Will he be all right?"

"He'll be all right," said Meg. "He has to be. He has a broken leg and a broken collar bone—again—he broke it once before." This made her smile a little, but she grew quickly sad again. "It's the head stuff they worry about, I guess. Everything else you can just fix."

We sat down by the edge of the pool and took off our sandals. We dangled our feet in the water. "I'm glad you're back," said Meg.

"I'm glad I'm back too," I said. It felt wonderful to be included in the circle of concern. It felt wonderful to be wanted, to hear that my being there mattered to Meg. We sat together quietly for a while, not talking. I didn't know if it would be appropriate for me to bring up my trip. I couldn't tell if Meg wanted to talk more about Stover or if she'd rather talk about something else.

The woman I'd seen earlier stuck her head out the back door.

"Meg," she called out. "Do you know where your mother keeps the rug attachment for the vacuum cleaner?"

"Somewhere in the basement," shouted Meg. "But it's not really working anymore."

"I thought that was your mother when I first saw her," I said.

"My mother's sister," said Meg. "Aunt Quig. Her last name is Quigley."

"Will she be staying here?"

"For a while, I guess. But not too long, we hope."

"She seems nice," I offered.

"Oh, she's nice, but she's the opposite of my mom. She'll try to have the whole house organized and shiny clean. When Mom was in the hospital when Theo was born she stayed with us and rearranged everything. She doesn't approve of the way Mom runs the house, so given the chance she puts everything the way she thinks it should be. It feels really odd around here with my parents and Stover away."

"You can come stay with me," I suggested. "We could camp out in the barn."

Meg considered this for a moment. Her face brightened. "I'd like to," she said, "but I better stay here. Mom might call from the hospital. And Theo needs me around. He's really upset. He misses Stover. This is scary for him. It's scary for us all," she added.

The screen door slammed behind us and I turned to see Jim walking toward us. He smiled at me. "Hi, Irene," he said. "You're back."

"Hi, Jim," I said.

"You guys going to swim?" he asked.

I looked at Meg. She shook her head. "Don't really feel like it," she said. "Unless you want to."

"No, not me."

Jim came and sat down beside me. I'd wondered which of us he'd sit next to. He put his feet in the water too.

"Welcome back," he said.

"Thanks."

"Got your postcards. How was the trip?" asked Jim.

"Pretty good. My sister had stuff planned for every day, but you'd need a couple of weeks to really see everything in Yellowstone."

The curved concrete molding along the pool was warm under my palms. I looked at my hand there, close to Jim's. I looked at his knee, close to mine. He was tan, and the hair on his legs was glinty gold in the sun. He moved his foot sideways underwater, so it was against mine. I inched my hand along the concrete so that the side of my hand was touching the side of his. He lifted his hand and put it flat on top of mine, his fingers slipped down between mine then bent around so he was holding tight. I shut my eyes. Meg couldn't see our hands; they were hidden between our bodies.

It was Meg's Aunt Quig who broke the spell. This time she wanted to know where there might be a new sponge for the sponge mop. Meg went in to help her find it. I thought maybe Jim would lift his hand from mine, but he didn't. He didn't seem to care if Meg saw or not.

"I'm really sorry about Stover," I said.

"Thanks," said Jim. "It's been a bummer."

"Meg says he'll be OK, though."

"He'll be OK," said Jim. "He's had the whole church putting in prayer time for him. And he's tough. If he'd been wearing a helmet, though, he wouldn't have gotten his head cracked open."

"Meg says the driver didn't stop."

"Nope, and if they ever catch the bastard I hope they lock him up for life."

"Did anybody see it happen?"

"Somebody did. But they didn't get a license number and all they could say about the car was that it was a silver grey, four-door sedan. Not much to go on."

"I hope they find him," I said.

"Yup," said Jim. He gave my hand a squeeze. I curled my fingers around his, and gave his hand a squeeze too.

A breeze came across the back of the house, stirring the water in the pool. It started in the shallow end, sending ripples toward the diving board, breaking up the flat surface of the water into small waves that caught the sunlight in each peak.

Jim released his hold on my hand and put his arm around my shoulder. "I'm glad you're here," he said.

I slipped my arm around his back and slowly let my weight shift so I was leaning against his body. I could hear his heart thumping against his ribs, and my heart thumping, as well, almost as if they were beating out a message to each other in code.

On the plane ride back from Wyoming I had thought about Jim kissing me and wondered when it might happen again. But this was something even better. And it was for only a second that I felt a little tug of guilt that I might be profiting this way because of what had happened to Stover.

chapter thirty

It wasn't until the next morning that I could get some time to talk alone with my grandfather. He was putting together an order to bring to Country Gardens.

"We're nearing the end of the summer season now," he said. "Soon it will be nothing but chrysanthemums." My grandfather shook his head.

"What's wrong with chrysanthemums?" I asked.

"Nothing's wrong with them. Sturdy, predictable plants. Sell well. But they just don't excite me much. With irises or clematis or hemerocallis—day lilies—you get endless interesting varieties." My grandfather pointed to the fields beyond the greenhouse, where rows of chrysanthemums were growing. "We can begin potting those up in another week," he said.

I lifted a tray of plants up onto the back of the truck and slid it far in. Bits of gravel on the bottom scratched along the metal floor. I wiped the dirt from my hands and leaned against the back of the truck.

"Grandpa," I began. "You'd never think of selling this place, would you?"

My grandfather put the tray of plants he was holding down on the ground.

"What makes you ask something like that, Irene?"

"I just wondered, that's all. I wouldn't want this place to turn into some subdivision, you know, houses all around."

"What has your father been saying to you?"

"Nothing. It's just that Jim said there was a developer who had his eye on the place and had been over here to talk with you."

My grandfather hoisted himself up on the back of the truck and patted the spot beside him. "Guess it's time then that you and I had a little talk," he said.

I climbed up and sat beside him. The metal of the tailgate was warm under my thighs.

"Truth is, I've had a pretty generous offer for this place and I've been giving it some thought recently."

"But Grandpa, you couldn't sell it!"

"I'm getting older. Have to think about retiring. Your father doesn't want to take over this business, live up here for good."

"Oh, he would. It's just Mom that wouldn't want to."

"That's right, she wouldn't—and so I have to make other plans."

"But what would you do? Where would you live?"

"They have some very nice communities around here, Irene. Condo units, everything taken care of for you."

I jumped off the back of the truck. "You couldn't do that!" I cried. "It would be awful. You'd hate it. Wouldn't you?"

"I can get used to anything."

"But why? Why would you have to? What's wrong with things just the way they are?"

"Nothing's wrong with them, Irene. Sometimes it's worth thinking about alternatives. Your father is my only child and you're my only grandchild. I have to think about you too."

"But I don't want you to sell this place. Ever. I want it to stay just the way it is."

"You can't have everything, sweetie."

"But couldn't I have this?"

My grandfather took off his wire-rimmed glasses and rubbed his eyes with both hands. He put his glasses carefully back on his face.

"You don't know what the future will be like. You can't say now what you'll be wanting then."

That was true. "But I'd want to have this as a choice," I said. "And what about now? I like to be here now. I don't want to give this up, not for anything."

My grandfather looked at me carefully. "You mean that, do you?"

"Yes," I said.

"I'll take that into consideration, then. I didn't know you felt that way. But I am getting older. I'm not going to be able to do this kind of work forever."

"But you're not too old for this now, Grandpa. You don't have to think about retiring now, do you?"

"No. I figure I have a few good years left in me yet," said my grandfather, smiling. He jumped off the truck and handed up the next tray of plants. "Going to drive with me to drop these off?" he asked.

"Sure," I said.

We filled the back of the truck with trays of plants and my grandfather flipped the tailgate shut. I climbed up into the cab beside him.

"I could drop you off at your friend's house, if you'd rather, on the way," he offered.

"That's OK," I said. "You can drop me off on the way back."

"How are things looking for Stover?" he asked.

"Better, I guess. But if they're doing CT scans does that mean there's a problem?"

"Not necessarily. They're pretty standard procedure after someone's had a concussion."

I felt better hearing him say that.

✳ ✳ ✳

Lucia was busy with a customer when we arrived. My grandfather gave her a little wave hello and we backed up the truck and started unloading. She came up and joined us after a while, smiling and shaking her head.

"Hello, Irene," she said. "Welcome back from your great adventure out West."

"Thank you," I said.

She gave my grandfather a little tug on his sleeve and he turned and smiled at her and gave her a kiss.

"Hello, you," she said.

"Somebody giving you a hard time?" my grandfather asked, pointing at the customer who was walking across the gravel to her car.

"Mary told her we didn't refund money on plants like that, the best we would do was store credit, but she insisted on seeing the owner. The plant had obviously been left out in the sun to scorch for a few weeks without water, but I gave her her money back."

"You're too soft, Lucia."

"Look who's talking," she said and laughed. She turned to me, smiling. "Your grandfather would give away plants for free to anyone who admired them."

When we were done unloading the truck we went inside for iced tea and raspberry muffins. The iced tea was in purple hand-blown glasses that were all ripply, with tiny air bubbles caught in the glass. My grandfather sat down and Lucia made his up for him. She put in four teaspoons of sugar, and balanced a lemon wedge perfectly on the lip.

"Tell me what you liked best," she said to me. "Tell me what was the highlight of your trip."

I thought over my week with Jenna. There had been so much packed in, but it seemed so far away now, as if it might have happened to another girl, not me.

"I liked the bison," I said. "There was one sitting by one of the hot springs. It was close as"—I pointed across the room—"that."

"Is your sister studying bison?" she asked.

"No, bighorn sheep. But they're farther north. We didn't see any of those."

"Did you see any bears?"

"Only two."

"When I went to Yellowstone when I was a girl, a million years ago, the bears came right up to your car. People fed them from the windows. Then they got to be dangerous and the parks department put a stop to it. Closed the dumps where the bears were being attracted to food. When I took my children to Yellowstone they were disappointed that the only bears they got to see were far off."

I hadn't thought about Lucia having had children. I knew she was a widow, but I hadn't really asked my grandfather much about her.

"We drove out west with Leland when he was a kid. Must have been around the same time you did," said my grandfather. "Went to Yellowstone. Fed the bears. Somewhere back at the house, Irene, I've got an album of that trip. Remind me to dig it out to show you."

"Maybe they were the exact same bears," I said.

My grandfather took a muffin "for the road" as he called it and offered me one too.

"Let me get you something to wrap those in," said Lucia, and we followed her to a cabinet in the back where she got some more paper napkins.

"No more cash refunds," my grandfather said, and he kissed Lucia good-bye.

"Good-bye, my dear," said Lucia to me, "come visit again soon."

I waved good-bye. We went out the back door of the shop this time. I was looking down, folding the napkin around the muffin Lucia had given me. When I looked up I saw a car parked on the side of the gravel driveway. It was a four-door, silver-grey sedan. I grabbed my grandfather's arm.

"Grandpa," I asked. "Do you know whose car that is?"

"It's a rental. Lucia's using it while her car is being repaired. Hers got done in at the A & P parking lot by some SUV. Did you see her car when you were here last?"

I shook my head. I was only half listening. "It's a big old Buick convertible. Hard to get the replacement parts for it."

We walked around the side of the shop, got in the truck, and started back home. My grandfather was in such an expansive mood he didn't realize that I wasn't talking. The iced tea was making me sick to my stomach. Or maybe it was the raspberry muffin I'd eaten.

"Could you pull over for a minute, Grandpa?" I asked.

"Are you all right?" he asked.

"I feel like I might throw up."

My grandfather slowed down and pulled off the side of the road. I opened the truck door and got out. It felt better to be standing on solid ground. We were near a house. There was a dog on a dog run between two trees who stood up when we stopped. I was afraid he was going to come over and bark at us, but it was an old dog, and after he looked us over and judged us not to be a threat, he sank back down again and laid his head on his paws.

After a while I felt better enough to get back into the truck.

"I'll take it easier around those curves," said my grandfather. "Still want me to drop you off at your friends' house?"

"I think I'd rather go home for now," I said.

I had an image stuck in my mind of when we'd arrived at Country Gardens: Lucia, giving my grandfather's sleeve a little tug, and the way he had smiled at her before he bent to kiss her. "Hello, you," she'd said to him. And yet, all along, there was that silver-grey sedan parked there behind Lucia's shop. It didn't make sense, none of it.

I thought of Jim's words: "If they ever catch the bastard I hope they lock him up for life." If only I'd had my grandfather drop me off at the Foxes' house on his way to Lucia's. If only we hadn't taken those extra muffins and gone out by the back door.

chapter thirty-one

My parents had gone into the city to see their lawyer and to meet with a financial counselor. This meeting had been my dad's idea, and I couldn't imagine much would come of it because my mom didn't think they needed, in her words, "some stranger telling us how to manage our lives." I'd overheard them arguing about it. They were attending some event in the evening afterward, and my dad hadn't wanted to go to that, even though my mom had insisted there'd be people there who could be useful to him. Obviously they'd struck a bargain between them.

I was tired and went to bed early. But I couldn't sleep. My grandfather was working on his accounts at the dining room table, using his old adding machine. Every time he hit the Add button it sounded as if there was a shooting gallery inside the machine, someone firing at all the numbers he'd just typed in. And although I tried to make myself not think about the things that were bothering me, I thought about them even more.

I got out of bed, put on my bathrobe, and walked quietly out of my bedroom. The hallway was dark, and the lights were off in the living room too. My grandfather was sitting in a pool of light under the chandelier over the dining room table. Joppy was stretched out on the floor beside him, sleeping. Joppy lifted his head slightly, took note of me, and then closed his eyes again.

There were stacks of paper spread over the table surface. I knew why my grandfather had waited until my parents were gone to do work here. My mom would never have approved of him using the table where we ate to do his accounts. She never let me spread out my homework on the dining room table in our apartment because she claimed it might ruin the finish. But it was more than that. Paperwork, she believed, belonged on desks.

I sat down quietly on the arm of the easy chair that was closest to the table. My grandfather hadn't noticed me yet; he was intent on his work. A tuft of hair was sticking out over his ear, as if he had been scratching his head, and his glasses had slid far down on his nose. He was adding columns of figures on the adding machine, then checking them against the columns in his ledger. He was a whiz at addition, and I wouldn't have been surprised if his own computations were more accurate than the machine's.

"Hi, Irene," he said when he saw me. "I thought you'd gone to bed long ago."

"I did," I said, "but I couldn't sleep."

"Miss those howling wolves, do you?"

I smiled. "Must be," I said.

"God I hate this paperwork," he said. "I put it off as long as I can, but it accumulates even faster, just to spite me. If you ever want to know why I decided not to practice law, you've got your answer right here."

I laughed a little. My grandfather pushed his glasses up and checked over another page of figures. Then he looked up at me again.

"Something on your mind, sweetie?" he asked.

I slipped down into the body of the chair and pulled my legs up under me.

"What if you knew something about somebody—or thought you might know something about somebody, but you weren't sure?"

My grandfather looked over the top of his glasses at me. "Yes?"

"What if someone might have done something, but you don't think they could have?"

"I think you better just tell me what's on your mind, Irene," said my grandfather. "I can't be much good as a listener if I don't know what you're talking about."

"What if telling about it could ruin everything?"

"It's usually not the telling that ruins things, Irene; it's the what's already happened. And not talking about it doesn't make it any less true."

It wasn't cold in the living room, but my feet felt cold. I pulled the bottom of my bathrobe down to cover them.

"The hit-and-run driver, the car that hit Stover—" I began.

"Yes?"

"It was just like Lucia's, the one she rented."

"How'd you know that?"

"Jim told me. Someone saw the car. Didn't get the license plate, though."

"And you're worried it might have been her car, that she might have been the driver."

I sucked in my lower lip and nodded.

"Well," said my grandfather, "I can see your dilemma now." He pushed the adding machine and pile of papers to the side and leaned back from the table. "Let's take a moment to look at the facts. OK?"

I nodded.

"Probably a lot of cars around that look like that, don't you think?"

"Yes. That's what I was thinking it had to be."

"Do you know when the accident happened?"

"Thursday. Late Thursday afternoon."

"Then there's nothing to worry about," said my grandfather. "If it was this past Thursday, it couldn't have been Lucia. Because all of last week she was up in Maine visiting her daughter and grandchildren. She'd rented the car when her Buick ended up in the shop, so she could make the trip up there as she'd planned. She didn't drive back until Saturday morning. So, do you feel better now?"

I sat still for a moment. Then I started laughing and somehow the laughing turned into crying, and they both were all mixed up. My grandfather got up from the table. He leaned over the chair and put his hands on either side of my face and kissed me on the forehead, upside down. Joppy came over and laid his head in my lap.

"See," my grandfather said, "sometimes things work out all right, don't they?"

When I could get my breath, I nodded. "They do," I said.

"There's something I need to ask you now," my grandfather said.

"Yes?"

"I'm aware that you don't know Lucia all that well, and don't have that much to go on, but from what you do know of her—do you think she's the kind of person who would hit a kid in the street and just keep driving on?"

"No, I don't think so."

"Good," said my grandfather. "That's what I hoped you would say."

chapter thirty-two

By the time the chrysanthemums were ready to be moved from their rows in the field to their three-quart pots, Stover was out of danger and back home. His most minor injury—a black eye—looked the most dramatic. His broken leg was in a Velcro cast, and at first he was stuck in a wheelchair, where he commanded the attention of the whole family, but he was quickly up and sprinting around on his crutches. People soon got used to his recovery and it was only Theo who still treated him like royalty and fetched things for him like his butler.

Jim and Meg worked with me in the field with the chrysanthemums. My grandfather said we were so good he didn't need to hire other help. It was Jim who worked the hardest and was most productive. Meg tried hard, but she got distracted. A red-tailed hawk circling overhead or a praying mantis on a leaf would catch her eye, and she'd get involved in watching it. I worked hard because of Jim—I wanted to show off to him that I could—but I often found myself watching him instead of digging the plants. When we were done we would run and plunge into the pond in our shorts and T-shirts, and float on our backs, and once, my grandfather took off his work boots and socks and jumped in with us.

The heat of the summer and the cool, inviting water of the pond and the hawk whistling overhead and Jim and Meg was where I was, but in the corner, a place I didn't turn my head to look, was something else. It didn't make it hurt less if we didn't talk about it, it was there: the coming of fall and the return to the city. When I saw the first leaf of a swamp maple start turning red, I wanted to tear it from the branch and hide it among the green.

I'll come back weekends, I told myself. I'll leave my room and my loft in the barn and everything just the way it is and come back every weekend. But it wouldn't be the same. All of us knew that.

There was still the unresolved business about my school. My parents thought it was resolved. Some temporary financial arrangement had been worked out so I could go back—some scholarship dredged up. But I didn't want to go back to my old school. I didn't want to face everyone there with things as they were. My dad still hadn't found a real job. He was doing some consulting work for someone who used to work for him—being paid nothing, my mom said, though what she meant was he wasn't earning anything like what they were used to. Nothing was said about how long the work would last, and what was going to happen next.

I went into the city with my parents on a Thursday morning. Neither Eve nor Frankie—nor any of my other friends—was back from their summer vacations. There wasn't a person I wanted to see, and there wasn't anything I wanted to do. I went because my mom insisted I go.

"You'll get to see the new apartment," she said, "and we'll do some shopping and have a nice dinner in a decent restaurant for a change."

I was nervous about seeing the apartment, but I wasn't sure why. Probably because my mom was so enthusiastic about it and my dad clearly wasn't. I picked up from the way he spoke that he didn't like this friend of my mom's, the owner. The apartment, a co-op, was being lent to them rent-free, but they would have to pay the monthly maintenance fees, which my dad said amounted to what it would cost them to rent something elsewhere.

The air in the city was hot and still, as if it was the same air, untouched, that we had left there when we'd moved in June. The apartment was in a small building near the East River. The elevator was tiny and slow, and even though the apartment was only on the third floor it took us a long time to get up there. We were all facing front, and I could see my dad's reflection in the highly polished brass. He looked like he was on the way to the dentist to have a tooth drilled.

The apartment smelled as if no one had opened a window for a hundred years. The foyer was paneled with mirrors. Some panels concealed closet doors, one a bathroom—a "powder room," my mom corrected me. The living room was sunken, down a curve of wide, carpeted steps. It was a huge, high-ceilinged room, with a fireplace on one wall. There were cherubs carved in the white stone, chubby, naked cherubs, who looked as if they longed to be released from the stone and set free into a blue sky.

"Isn't that a remarkable fireplace?" said my mom. "They had it brought back from Italy, piece by piece."

The furniture in the room was all antiques, the pale, spindly kind. There wasn't anything that you'd want to sit down on. My dad lowered himself carefully on a chair and unbuttoned the top of his shirt. I walked across the room. The wall was glass brick, two stories high, disconcerting because it looked as if you were peering through someone else's glasses. On either flank were real windows that you could see out of. I looked down at the street. The brownstones across the way were dark and silent.

My mom was eager to take me on a tour of the rest of the apartment. There was a large, formal dining room with a chandelier that would crush the table beneath it if it fell. The kitchen was black and chrome, and looked as if no one had ever cooked a meal there. My mom led me on through the master bedroom, through a dressing room, to a bathroom that was all dark green marble, with an enormous tub, and an exercise corner.

"Look," said my mom, opening a cabinet which turned out to be a refrigerator. "It's designed for champagne, but you can keep soda in here."

The bedroom was decorated in the palest of pinks. It looked as if no one had ever walked on the carpeting even with bare feet, let alone shoes, or ever touched the bedspread on the bed. My mom tapped the pink marble top of a chest of drawers. It was a four-drawer chest that bulged out in front, as if it were pregnant, but rested on delicate-looking feet.

"French," my mom said. "Isn't it gorgeous?"

"Where's the other bedroom?" I asked, looking around.

"There's only this one."

"But where am I going to sleep?"

"Don't worry, darling," said my mom. "We have it all figured out. You're going to sleep here, and Daddy and I are going to sleep in the dining room, on those two day-beds in the alcove. We'll use the dressing room here, which has oodles of closet space."

I looked around the bedroom. All the furniture was gilded and fragile-looking. I couldn't imagine spending a night in it, let alone a year.

"But where will I keep my things? Where will I do my homework?"

"We'll get you a nice desk," my mom said, "the kind that's like a little office that all folds up."

"But what about all my stuff?" I asked. "My chair, my books, my posters. You're getting my stuff out from storage, aren't you?"

"Not while we're here, not for a while."

I walked back into the living room.

"Daddy—" I began.

My dad looked up at me. I could see in his face that he knew how I'd feel about the apartment, that he'd known all along. That's why he hadn't wanted to be here. He knew that this wasn't an apartment for the three of us. He knew there was no place in this apartment that would work for someone my age. He wouldn't say anything in my mom's defense, but he wouldn't say anything against her, either. There wasn't any point in me saying anything. My mom had rationalized the problems with the apartment because it was the kind of place that she wanted to live in, and she felt she'd made the ultimate sacrifice by giving me the master bedroom. My dad knew why the apartment wasn't right for us, but he'd let my mom have her way. Why did it always have to be that way with him? Why couldn't he ever stick up for me?

chapter thirty-three

I sink down in the seat on the train and press my face against the cool window. All the way to the station, I ran and walked until I caught my breath, then ran again. I made it ten minutes before the train was scheduled to leave, enough time to buy my ticket and board. I keep picturing my dad bursting into the train car, looking around for me, his hair stuck to his forehead with sweat, his tie askew, although I know it will be hours at least before my mom gets back and sees the note, hours before she'll tell him what I've done.

There are very few other passengers on the train—people aren't heading home from work yet. I make myself small so I won't be noticed, so no one will ask me what I'm doing. It seems like the train will never move and I wonder if something's wrong, if maybe I'm on the wrong train, one that isn't ever going to leave the station. But I don't want to get up and ask anyone.

I don't want to call attention to myself. I press my feet against the back of the seat in front of me. "Move," I whisper to the train. "Please, move."

Finally, just when I've almost given up hope, there's that long sad cry, "All aboard!" and the train closes itself up, stirs, and starts edging forward. It lurches, then comes to a complete halt. Then starts moving again.

I've never taken the train by myself before. I've flown across the whole United States by myself, but that was different—there was Jenna waiting for me at one end, my dad waiting for me at the other. But no one is waiting for me now. I'm on a train I'm not supposed to be on, going someplace where no one is expecting me. No one in the world knows where I am right now. And if no one knows, it's as if, in a way, I don't exist.

The tunnel is long and dark. The train seems to be crawling its way underground, searching for a way to the mouth. I wonder if it's possible for it to get lost here in this underworld, if we could just keep inching along in the dark, forever. Every now and then there's a small red or dim yellow light along the way, and once we pass a ladder that leads up into the blackness. At last there's a hint of real light ahead, and almost too suddenly we're outside. I blink in the daylight. I'd almost forgotten that it's the middle of a summer afternoon, and even though we're in the city, there's still sunshine here.

The train picks up speed. And now the city flies by me, building after building, and I feel so relieved to be moving, to be free, to be doing something that I want, on my own, for the first time, I almost cry.

The conductor comes by and takes my ticket. He gives me a questioning look, but I just smile up at him quickly and then look down at my book. It seems amazing I can get away with it, amazing that he just moves on down the aisle.

I've never done anything like this before in my life. Never run away. Or maybe it isn't running away. Maybe it's running toward. The conductor sings out the station names, and it's my trip into the city in reverse. The farther we get from the city, the less anxious I feel. I look at my watch. My parents still don't know that I've left. I'm absolutely safe. I don't mind the train ride now; in fact, it would be OK with me if it goes on forever. When the conductor sings out the name of my station, it sounds as if he's singing just to me. The train slows as it comes into the station and at the end of the platform the lettered name of the town seems like a welcome home sign. I make my way up to the front of the car as the train huffs to a stop. The conductor sets out a metal stepping block and gives me a hand down. It's early afternoon, and the platform is hot and sunny. The train lingers at the station, and I duck into the shady coolness of the station house because I don't want the conductor to see there's no one here to meet me. When I hear the train starting up again I step out onto the platform. It's a short train, not like the two dozen cars that are on at rush hour, and no one has boarded at my station. I watch the train as it pulls out of the station. It lumbers along at first, then gathers speed. After it's out of sight, around a bend, I can hear its whistle. I know it's a warning as it crosses a roadway, but I imagine it's the train saying good-bye to me, wishing me well.

✳ ✳ ✳

From the phone booth outside the station, I called my grandfather. I hadn't really thought about what I'd do if he wasn't home, since I was pretty sure he hadn't planned to go anywhere that day. But when he didn't answer the phone I realized that although he had an extension in the greenhouse, if he was working out in the field, he probably wouldn't hear it ring.

I hung up the phone and looked around. The street was empty. It was too far to walk to my grandfather's house, but I might not have any choice. I called again and let the phone ring and ring. Finally I decided to call Meg and Jim. They might have an idea of what I could do, and there was always the chance their mom was driving into town for some errand and could come pick me up. And I wanted to hear their voices; I wanted to tell them what I had done. But I got their answering machine with Theo's all-too-familiar message, so I hung up.

A man who worked for the railroad came along the sidewalk. He seemed to be looking at me, so I got out the phone directory and started leafing through. Then I tried my grandfather again. I counted to ten rings. Then I hung up, called again, and let it ring. I counted to fourteen. I looked out in the parking lot. My parents' car was there, where they'd left it when we drove to the station that morning. It seemed crazy that it was there, not being used, and I was stuck, without a ride.

I thought about the walk to my grandfather's house. The station was at the far end of town. It was about an hour's bike ride from the center of town to my grandfather's house. It would take about twice as long by foot. If I left then, I'd still be at my grandfather's house before my parents arrived, though I wasn't sure I'd make it before they called.

I called my grandfather's number again and willed him to hear the phone. But he didn't pick up. Then it occurred to me that maybe he'd gone to see Lucia. I found Country Gardens under "nurseries" in the yellow pages.

Lucia said my grandfather wasn't there. She wondered where I was, and when I told her, she misunderstood and thought he was supposed to pick me up at the station and had forgotten to.

"It's not quite like that," I said, and I began to explain that my grandfather didn't know I'd be coming back this early, and he wasn't answering his phone.

"Are you alone at the station?" she asked me.

"Well, yes, I am."

"Wait right there, Irene. I'll be over to get you in five minutes," and she hung up before I could say anything in protest.

I waited on the bench outside the station. Lucia picked me up in her big, old Buick convertible. "First things first," she said to me. "Are you all right?"

"I'm fine," I said. I could understand why Lucia was concerned, but it was hard not to sound impatient.

"Does anyone know you're here?"

"Not really," I said.

"Where are you supposed to be?"

"In the city."

"Enough questions," said Lucia, and she smiled at me. "I'll drive you to your grandfather's, and if he's not there, if you like, you can come back to the shop with me."

My grandfather's pickup was there in the driveway, so I was sure he was home.

"Say hello for me," said Lucia.

I thanked Lucia and waved good-bye. I went into the house.

"Grandpa?" I called. No one answered. I·looked out the window and spotted him way out in back. I went into my room and changed out of my city clothes, then I started walking out across the field. Joppy came bounding up and announced my arrival.

My grandfather had been bending over, digging. He turned around, both hands on the shovel.

"Hi, sweetie," he said. "Didn't expect you back this early."

"Hi, Grandpa," I said. I bent down to pat Joppy.

"Thought you were spending the day in the city, having dinner there tonight."

I didn't say anything.

"Irene," he asked. "Is everything all right?"

"Everything's all right, Grandpa. Sorry I surprised you."

"I'm just surprised your parents decided to make such a short day of it."

"They didn't," I said.

My grandfather looked up toward the house, and back at me.

"They're not here," I said. "They're still in the city. I came back on my own."

"They sent you back?"

I shook my head.

"They know you're back?

"They will soon. I left a note," I said.

My grandfather let out a low whistle. "I think you've got a bit of explaining to do," he said. He kicked the dirt off his shovel, slung it over his shoulder, and we started walking back to the house. He called Joppy, who'd run off farther into the field.

I told my grandfather all about the apartment. I told him I had persuaded my mom to let me go off shopping on my own and she'd given me a set of keys. The plan was we'd meet back at the apartment, then join my dad at a restaurant for dinner. But instead of going shopping I'd walked a few blocks downtown and then back to the apartment. I looked at the train timetable, wrote a quick note and left it on the table in the front hall, and raced off to the station.

My grandfather took off his glasses, wiped them on his shirttail, held them up to the light, gave them another wipe and put them back on.

"So, what is this all about, Irene. What is it you want to do?"

"I want to stay here with you, Grandpa. I don't want to move back to the city and live in that apartment. I want to go to school here."

"What about your old school? I thought you loved it."

"I did, when I was there, back then, but I don't want to be there now. Dad said 'special arrangements' would be made. I know what that means. It would be like they were taking me in as a charity case."

"But there are other girls who are there on scholarship. There's nothing shameful about that, Irene. Nothing shameful about not being wealthy enough to pay private school tuition."

"But it's different for us. It's not that my parents are really poor, it's just that they screwed up."

"Irene!"

"I'm sorry, Grandpa, but it's true. The girls who get scholarships are girls who really need them. It's different for them. How can I be on scholarship when Mom shops at Bonwit Teller?"

My grandfather let out a sigh. "I can come up with the money for your school tuition, Irene," he said. "You don't have to be on scholarship."

"But I don't want that, Grandpa. I don't want you to have to sell off land, or borrow against it. The public school here is a great school. I'd like to go here."

"What about all your friends in New York? Eve, Frankie."

I waited. "I'll miss them," I said. "But I have friends

here too now, Grandpa. The thing is, I really want to stay here. I want to live in this house. I want to live with you."

"What about your parents?"

I turned away.

"Irene, they're your parents. They love you."

"Right," I said.

My grandfather took me by the shoulders and turned me around.

"They do love you," he said.

"So if they love me so much how come they never think about me? If they love me so much how come they always decide what they want to do and then work me into their plans? I never have any say about anything. They sell our apartment, put all my things in storage, and move me up here. I had no choice about that. I get settled here and I make friends and I like it here, then they get this fancy little apartment in New York and expect me to just pick up and move back with them. They never ask me how I feel about anything. They never ask me what I want. Mom just does what she wants to do and Daddy just goes along with her. He never stands up to her about anything. Never."

"He's not in a good position to stand up to your mother now. He feels he's let her down. He's depressed."

"Well, I'm sorry about that. But what about me? Don't I count for anything?"

"Of course you count, Irene; you count very much."

My grandfather took me in his arms and hugged me close.

"Please let me stay with you," I asked. "Please."

"It's not for me to say, sweetie. It's your parents' decision."

"But you'd let me live with you, wouldn't you?"

"Of course I would. If you want to stay here—maybe for this school year, until things are settled and your parents have a more permanent place to live—that would be fine with me. But it's not up to me, Irene. You'll have to convince them."

"But you're on my side, aren't you, Grandpa?"

"There are no sides, Irene. All that matters is what's best for you."

"But isn't this best for me? Isn't it best for me to stay here for now?"

My grandfather didn't say anything for a minute.

"Isn't it?" I asked again.

"We'll see," he said at last.

chapter thirty-four

They called when they read my note. I knew they'd
be calling, so when the phone rang I made my grandfather
pick it up. It was my dad who called, and I leaned against
the wall in the living room, out of sight, while my grandfather spoke with him. I could imagine my dad's side of the
conversation, imagine my mom standing by the phone,
overseeing the call. I could imagine my dad telling my
grandfather how upset my mom was.

"Yes, Leland," my grandfather said, in his calm, soft
voice. "I can see how she would be."

When he hung up, I stepped around into the hall. He was
standing with his back to me and he saw me in the mirror over
the hall table. He turned around. "They should be back by
eight," he said. They're going to get takeout to eat on the train
on the way back. Guess we should get us some dinner now."

I didn't feel like eating, but my grandfather made spaghetti and a big salad for me. I nibbled on the red peppers in the salad. My grandfather's peppers are sweet and juicy, and I like to puncture the skin with my teeth and bite down into them. But I couldn't do much more with the spaghetti than push it around on my plate, twirl it on my fork, and let it slip off again.

All of the courage I had been feeling, all of the certainty about what I had done, was gone now. I could picture my parents on the train, my mom sitting up straight in her seat, her lips pressed together, my dad not saying much, his fingers drumming on the armrest until my mom told him to stop.

I knew what time the train was getting in. I knew how long it would take for my parents to get to the house from the train station. I had my eye on the clock, waiting. The house was silent. My grandfather was at his desk, going through seed catalogs. I was reading a book, but I wasn't really reading. I was running through the progress of my parents' trip in my mind. I pictured the train coming to a stop at the station and them stepping down onto the platform. I pictured them walking to the car, my dad unlocking it, holding the door open for my mom while she got in. I pictured my dad starting the engine, letting the car warm up for a second before he backed out of the space. I pictured the car pulling out onto West Main Street, waiting at the light, turning left on Hillside Avenue on the bridge that went over the railroad tracks.

Suddenly Joppy sprang up from his place on the floor beside my grandfather's chair. He'd heard the car in the driveway before I did. My calculations were all off. The train must have gotten in early, or else my dad had driven the car faster than anyone had ever driven it before.

I pulled back into my corner of the sofa, but kept my eye on the front hall. My grandfather met my parents at the door. He said he had someplace he needed to go in town—I assume he was going to Lucia's house—but my mom caught him by the sleeve.

"Arthur," she said. "You're part of this. I don't think you should be running off now."

"Very well, Andrea," my grandfather said. "But this is really between Irene and the two of you. I'm here for her; this place is here for her, but what you decide to do is entirely up to you."

"How can it be just up to us with you telling her she should stay here in the country, not come back to the city with us?"

"I haven't been telling Irene anything," said my grandfather. "All I've been doing is listening to her."

I thought my mom was going to hit my grandfather. Her face got red, her neck got red, and her hand moved up toward her face. But instead of shouting or hitting, she burst into tears.

My dad put his arm around her and steered her into the living room. He helped her sit down on the ottoman by my grandfather's big chair. She sat down, her shoulders slumped, and put her face into her hands.

I went up to her and kneeled on the floor by the ottoman. "I'm sorry, Mom," I said. I wasn't sure what I was sorry for—not for what I had done, I couldn't be sorry for that—but I felt sorry anyway. I wasn't used to seeing my mom like this, small and curled over, her shoulders heaving, even after the crying had stopped.

When she looked up at me she said, "First Jenna, now you."

"What do you mean, first Jenna?" I asked.

"You didn't know this; you were too little then to know what was going on," said my dad, "but when Jenna was your age she chose to live with her father, rather than live with us."

"I thought you shipped her off to live with him, that it wasn't convenient for you to have her living with you then."

My mom's face went white.

"Where did you ever get that idea?" she whispered.

"Jenna."

"Is that what she told you?" she asked. "Is that what she thought?"

"Well, something like that," I said.

"It wasn't like that," said my mom. "It wasn't like that at all. Your father was working with the London branch of the company when we were first married. We had a flat there. Jenna was a teenager; she didn't want to be living abroad. Her father was here, in the United States, in a nice town with a good school. It seemed best for her to live with him during the school term, spend her vacation time with us. Then, after you were born and we were back living in New

York, she wanted to continue living with her father. She'd made friends in that town; her life was there. I gave in. It wasn't that we didn't want her, Irene. It was never that."

I thought about Jenna and that night in the little cabin in Yellowstone. It was a night so far away, it could have been on the other side of the world. Was it real? Was it possible that that little cabin was still there, empty of us, but still there? I thought about what Jenna had told me then, about what my mom was saying now. Who knew the way things had really been? Who could be sure what people had really wanted then? It was all so muddied now.

No one was saying anything. I looked at my grandfather. He was looking at my dad. They looked at each other for a few seconds.

"This isn't about Jenna," said my dad at last. "This is about Irene."

"Irene running off. Taking the train up here alone when we thought she was safely back in the apartment." My mom turned to me now. "Why did you do that?" she asked. But her voice wasn't angry; it was only sad. I had expected her to be angry. This was harder.

"I couldn't stay in that apartment," I said. "I just had to get out of the city. I just had to get back here."

"Why didn't you tell us?"

"I didn't know... I mean..."

"Why haven't you been talking to us?"

I couldn't say anything to that.

"Maybe we haven't been that easy to talk to," said my dad.

chapter thirty-five

I've never had trouble talking before. In fact, talking is one of the few things I did all the time, and always thought I did pretty well. But now it was as if I couldn't really talk; I couldn't explain anything. My dad sat on the chair behind my mom. She sat where she was on the ottoman, and I sat on the floor in front of them. My mom's shoulders were still slumped, as if she no longer had the energy to maintain her usual posture.

My mom wanted me to tell them what I thought I wanted, but when she pressed me to explain the "why" about things, I found myself saying just "because" and not being able to get much farther. The word "because" became everything—everything I couldn't really explain.

She didn't understand about the apartment at all. It wasn't as if they were having me sleep in the dining room, she pointed out—they were giving me the master bedroom. And they'd never invade my privacy—they'd just be keeping a few things in one of the dressers there. And of course I'd be able to use the living room when my friends came over. And all they'd have to do was put aside a few of the more fragile pieces and there'd be no reason why I couldn't have parties there. And they certainly could take some of my things out of storage if there was anything special I really wanted.

The way she put everything, it all seemed so reasonable. None of my arguments seemed very good anymore. I didn't really want what was in storage. Anyone listening would wonder what was wrong with me, wonder what it was that I wanted. I sounded silly, even to my own ears. It sounded as if what I was unhappy about was that I'd have to handle the spindly antique chairs with care.

When I brought up the subject of my school and how I felt about getting financial aid, my mom flashed a look at my grandfather.

"I told Irene I was ready to raise the money for tuition," said my grandfather, "if being on scholarship there made her feel uncomfortable."

"But I don't want Grandpa to be selling this land," I said.

"There's acres and acres," said my mom. "All that was under consideration was a small building lot, at the far end of the property."

"But I don't want the farm to be touched. Any of it. I love this place," I said. "And I want to stay here. I don't want to go back to my old school."

My mom shook her head and let out a sigh. She held her palm in the air and turned to my dad, expecting him to take over while she caught her breath.

But my dad surprised us all. At least he surprised her and he surprised me. Instead of picking up my mom's chain of arguing, he turned to her and took up my case. He sounded as if he were a lawyer paraphrasing what a witness had just said in a way that the jury could understand.

"What Irene has been asking for, Andie, isn't to live up here forever. What she's asking for is to stay up here this coming year. She's happy here; she likes this place, this town. She's made good friends. The public school here is excellent. I think it's a good idea for her, if she wants to do it. She'll spend weekends in the city, with us. By the end of the year I'll certainly have the right job with a good salary. Then we can find an apartment of our own, claim our things from storage. In a year we can turn our lives around, Andie."

My mom looked at my dad. The muscles in her neck were tight.

"How can you say this, Leland?" she asked. "We discussed all of this. We went over all of it on the train coming back here. You agreed with me then! What happened to turn you around this way?"

"I've been listening to Irene," he said. "I've been learning about what she's feeling. I've been seeing things I hadn't seen before."

My mom opened her mouth and closed it again. For

the first time that I could remember she seemed to have nothing to say.

My dad leaned forward and stroked the sides of her head, pushing the hair back over her ears.

"What I've been hearing from Irene, Andie," said my dad, speaking softly now, "is how little control she's felt she's had over her life this past year, how things kept happening to her and she was never given a chance to make any decisions for herself. Whatever the merit of this plan of hers—and I think it's a plan that has considerable merit—the important aspect is that she's thought things through, taken charge of her own life. Everyone needs to feel they have some control over their own life. Andie, you, of anyone, should know that well. Irene is growing up. I think it's time we gave her that chance."

My dad, in his calm, reasoned way, sounded like a man who could persuade anyone of anything. I saw then why he had been successful at his job, why he'd be successful once again.

Not only had he stood up for me, at last, but he'd seen me even better than I'd seen myself.

My mom took his hand, gripped it, and held it against her chest. She looked small and old and tired. Her mascara had smudged, leaving black crescents under her eyes, and the flesh on either side of her mouth sagged. She looked at me, without speaking, and it was a way she had never looked at me before.

"All right then, Leland, if you think so," is what, at last, she said.

chapter thirty-six

In the morning, before my parents were awake, I went out to the barn and climbed up to my loft. Later in the day it would get hot up here, but now the sun was only just starting to reach in through the open barn doors below me and it was still as cool as evening. I re-arranged my things in the bookcase, leaving one of the top pear boxes empty for new books. When school started in a few weeks, I would do my homework up here. The barn wasn't heated in the winter, but winter was a long way away.

The small window over the bookcase looked out toward the pond and the fields. A stone wall rambled along the far edge of the fields, as if it were holding back the woods beyond. I thought of the view from my old room in our penthouse in the city: lower Manhattan—apartment buildings like mine and office buildings—and a slice of the Hudson River. I wondered who lived in my room now, looking out at my old view.

I turned from the window, stretched out on the velvet loveseat, and slung my feet over the arm. My big striped armchair was in storage, waiting for me to reclaim it, and my brass canopy bed was there too, stacked up in pieces, waiting to be restored and made whole. They'd just have to wait a while longer. The loft had that comforting barn smell of the day just beginning. I ran my hand along the seat cushion, smoothing the velvet one way, then rubbing it back toward me, against the nap. A darker gold hand-print against the gold.

The night before, my mother had come into my bedroom just before I had gone to sleep. "I just want you to know that if you change your mind, you don't have to stay here. You can always come and live with us in the city and go back to your old school."

"I know," I said.

"Anytime," my mother added, just as she left my room.

I didn't think it was very likely that I would change my mind. But I didn't tell my mother that.

I heard someone coming into the barn now, and I got up and looked over the side of the hayloft.

"Thought I might find you in here," said my grandfather. "Ready for some breakfast?"

"OK," I said. I climbed down the ladder.

"I thought we might have a little picnic out in the *Holden Caulfield*." My grandfather had a basket in his hand.

"Breakfast in a canoe?" I asked.

"Worth trying once."

We took the paddles and walked down to the pond. We flipped over the canoe, and I got in first and made my way carefully to the bow. My grandfather handed the basket to me before he got in.

"I already ate," he said, "so keep it down at your end. You can let me do the paddling." I turned around and sat on the bottom of the canoe, facing my grandfather, and used the cane seat between us as a table. Breakfast was buttered toast, slices of cheese, and a bowl of raspberries.

"Just picked those," said my grandfather. "You might want to check them for insects before you pop them in your mouth."

The raspberries were dewy and soft and sweet. I made myself eat them just one at a time so I wouldn't eat them too fast.

"I brought you out here because there's something I want to ask you about," he said. "But first I want to hear how you're feeling about last night."

"OK," I said. "It's a little scary, but that doesn't mean it's not what I want to do."

"I can see that."

"Mom made a big point of telling me that I could change my mind anytime and it was OK with her."

My grandfather tilted his head, waiting.

"I'm not changing my mind," I said.

"If you ever feel you might want to," said my grandfather, "it's OK with me too."

"I know that," I said.

We did a slow circle around the pond, moving from patches of sunlight to places where overhanging maples cast their shadows. I closed my eyes in the sunlight and held a raspberry in my mouth, not chewing it, just pressing it against the roof of my mouth with my tongue, tasting it.

I opened my eyes. "What was it you wanted to ask me?"

My grandfather looked embarrassed. He laid the paddle across the canoe and leaned forward on it.

"I was thinking last night that since your parents will be going back to the city—and if you still want to live out here—

"I *do*," I said.

"I figured it might be nice for you to have a woman living in the house, not just me, and I wondered what you thought about my inviting Lucia."

I sat up. "That would be great," I said.

My grandfather was rubbing his chin in a way that I knew meant that he wasn't quite done. "Here's the thing, though," he said. "I figure if I'm asking her to live with us, I should offer her a title."

"You mean ask her to marry you?"

"That's more or less the kind of thing I had in mind."

"Grandpa, that's wonderful! How long have you wanted to marry her?"

"Since the day we met."

"When was that?"

"Six years ago. October 13th."

"You've been waiting six years!"

"Guess it just took me a while. Hearing you last night, I figured it was about time I showed some courage too."

※ ※ ※

After my grandfather went back to the house, I stayed out in the canoe, paddling lazily now and then. It still smelled like morning and the day before me seemed wonderfully long, as if it would go on forever. Sometime later, I would go over to the Foxes and tell them—Jim and Meg—my good news, and I would call Jenna and tell her too. But not yet. I still wanted to get used to it myself. I laid down my paddle and sat back down in the bottom of the canoe. I leaned my head back against the seat and looked up at the sky. A speck of silver, an airplane, was moving across the blue, leaving behind it a thread of white. Soon the plane was out of sight, and finally its trail had vanished too. I reached over the side of the canoe and dangled my hand toward the water. My fingertips just touched the surface. There was a breeze coming across the pond. I let it take the canoe and move it gently, turn it one way and then another.

※ ※ ※

The wedding takes place on an early October day that's so warm it feels like summer.

Lucia wears a dress that's the blue of her eyes and the sky, and she wears a crown of clematis terniflora, sweet autumn clematis, in her silver-grey hair.

"It's the only reason I agreed to get married," she says, smiling. "I always wanted an excuse to wear a crown of these flowers."

I helped her make it, snipping long sections of the vine and wrapping it into a circle, weaving in shorter, flower-filled stems all around. The flowers are tiny white stars, and when I place it on Lucia's head, she looks like a woodland fairy.

My grandfather is wearing a blue work shirt, ironed, with a tie and seersucker jacket. Lucia tucks a sprig of clematis in the lapel and kisses my grandfather's shoulder.

A justice of the peace, who is a faithful customer at Country Gardens, is going to do the official part of the wedding, but the ceremony is something my grandfather and Lucia put together. I am the bridesmaid. My mom took me shopping in the city for my dress. There wasn't much she could do to help out with arrangements for the wedding—Lucia and my grandfather wanted it to be simple and did the preparations themselves—so she threw herself into the enterprise of finding me the perfect dress. It's one we both like. She's pleased because she thinks I can wear it on other occasions, like parties at school. I don't want to disappoint her, so I don't tell her that at parties everyone just wears jeans.

A friend of Lucia's plays a tune on the pennywhistle, while Lucia and I walk around on the path, to the far side of the pond. I help Lucia get into the canoe. Meg and I decorated it with laurel branches and bunches of purple asters, white phlox, and pink chrysanthemums. The surface of the pond is so clear and flat it's a perfect reflection of the sky, and when I shove the canoe out into the water, it looks like a flower garden parting the clouds.

I walk on around the pond, back to the field where everyone is standing in a semicircle by the water. Jenna is here—my grandfather sent her the plane tickets—and my parents, and Lucia's daughter and family, and friends of Lucia and my grandfather, and Meg, Jim, Stover, Lolly, and Theo. Theo is the ring bearer, and he's gripping the box so tightly his fist is white. Jim catches my eye and smiles.

Lucia paddles slowly across the pond to the birdsong of the pennywhistle. My grandfather is waiting on the shore. He pulls the canoe up on the grass, lifts Lucia out, and sets her on the ground beside him. Joppy wags his tail furiously with pleasure. I can tell he's dying to jump up and greet the arriving bride, but he manages to restrain himself and stay sitting where my grandfather asked him to.

Lucia hands me her bouquet and takes my grandfather's hands. The bouquet is filled with flowers from all of Lucia's favorite plants from the greenhouse. The smell of heliotrope fills the afternoon with its sweetness.

My grandfather turns to the circle of guests. "Thank you all for being here today," he begins. He turns to Lucia. "Especially you."

Theo, mistaking this for his cue, springs forward from his place beside Meg and thrusts the ring box out to my grandfather.

"Here they are," Theo says triumphantly. "And I didn't drop the box. Not even once."

Everyone laughs. But it's my parents' laughter beside me that I hear the best. They have their arms around each other and they look happy, really happy. It's been so long since I've seen them this way, I've almost forgotten.

Joppy, who may not understand why we are all laughing, can restrain himself no longer. He dashes around in gleeful circles, barking in the sunshine.

acknowledgments

My thanks to my agent, Edward Necarsulmer IV, indefatigable, dedicated, and wise, and to my wonderful editor, Andrew Karre, who understood Irene from the very start.

Thanks to my writing circle: Barbara Diamond Goldin, Anna Kirwan, Patricia MacLachlan, Lesléa Newman, Ann Turner, Ellen Wittlinger, and Jane Yolen, and to my Cushman Café writing buddies: Betsy Hartmann, Karen Osborn, Julian Olf, Robert Redick, Dan Bullen, and Linda Roghaar, my friend Elaine Lasker von Bruns, and my family, especially Artemis Demas Roehrig, my superb reader, and Matthew Roehrig, who makes all my books possible.

I am grateful for the continuing support of Mount Holyoke College.

Special thanks to Brian, Alice, Leah, and Emma McGowan, of Blue Meadow Farm.